MW01128814

Across the Wilderness

By

Pamela Ackerson

Across the Wilderness
By *Pamela Ackerson*

Cover Art: Jean Joachim

Disclaimer:

This is a work of fiction. Any relation to real people, living or dead, are creations of the author's imagination.

Chapter One

Leaning against the verandah doorframe, Karen watched the delivery men struggle with the awkward and heavy feather mattress she had re-upholstered. The ornate bed was large and high off the carpeted floor. She had fallen in love with it the moment she and her friend, Bonnie, had seen it at the estate sale.

The antique maple bed and steps matched her furnishings in the room to perfection. For some unknown reason, she had decided that this room be furnished with antiques, right down to her eagle photographs in ornately carved frames. Normally, Karen was comfortable with anything and everything contemporary. It wasn't until the past year that she started replacing her bedroom furniture with antiques.

After the men left, she spent the afternoon organizing and rearranging the rest of the bedroom. Nodding her head in agreement with herself, she looked about the room with a critical eye. It was almost as if the bed was the last piece of the puzzle. Its headboard was strategically placed against the wall with the two windows from floor to ceiling on each side. A slight breeze moved the French lace curtains. The bed faced the verandah; the armoire to the right of the bed; the bureau and matching vanity to its left. Smiling, the room looked comfortable and inviting.

Hot and exhausted, she laid on the bed for an afternoon nap. She felt herself relaxing against the cool linen sheets. The bed, soft and enveloping, hugged her as she dozed into a restful sleep. Karen felt as if she was floating on water and then upward as if she was flying. It was an exquisite sensation. In the dream, she closed her eyes and felt the freedom of gliding peacefully in the sky. Opening her eyes, she surveyed her surroundings as she drifted back to the earth. Karen felt the dirt and grass beneath her bare feet.

Karen's peaceful dream was interrupted by the man who stood before her. The threatening and menacing look on the man's face had burst the serenity from moments before.

One moment she was reeling in the luxury of the soft bed and then, without warning, she was staring at an extremely handsome and virile looking Indian. As she watched his face, she could see a look of complete astonishment that had quickly turned to anger.

He looked quite perturbed at the intrusion.

Standing Deer was getting ready to eat his morning meal when out of the blue heavens she appeared. All of a sudden, there she was; a very beautiful woman, just barely able to reach his shoulders. This white woman had long wavy hair with curls cascading down from her shoulders to her waist, like a waterfall. The rays of sunshine through the clouds and sky cast its light upon it causing her hair to sparkle and shimmer. There were so many streaks of colors in it that he wasn't sure what color to call it. It appeared to have all the colors of autumn leaves one saw in the mountains just before the winter snows. He wanted to reach over and touch its beauty.

How ironic that she would appear just when he thought the whole trip was a waste of his valuable time. He'd been scouting for days and had not seen any Pawnee war parties or scouts. This woman, dressed in clothing he had never seen before, was quite different from other white women. What has the Great Spirit planned for him by bringing this woman to him? Where did she come from? How did she get here without him seeing her? He didn't see a horse. Confused, Standing Deer wondered how she entered the campsite without him seeing her.

He didn't move, nor did Standing Deer want to move. If he scared her, she might leave in the same way she arrived. From his own experiences and those of others, he knew white women were cowards. They tended to get very skittish when they were around Indians. He didn't want to scare her away. He wanted answers to his questions.

The training of a Hunkpapa warrior prepared Standing Deer to be ready for anything. This was different. It was magical how she appeared before his eyes. Standing Deer could feel his palms sweating, and his heart beating faster. He felt an attraction he hadn't allowed himself to feel in years. What kind of spell had she cast over him?

Standing Deer was thorough as he stood silently admiring and observing her. She was indeed in strange attire, with practically nothing covering her body. This woman with the colorful hair and strange clothes didn't appear to be shaken by his presence. Grinning, her attire didn't leave much to the imagination. She was quite striking; her body was well-formed and well-endowed. She appeared to be strong and healthy for a white woman. It pleased him to see the muscles throughout her arms and legs. Yes, she was quite a specimen. This woman was a strong one.

She would be able to work hard, stand her own ground among the other captives and possibly even among the Indian women of the tribe. She would surely bring him good fortune and many horses when he traded her to the Cheyenne. He should bring this white woman back to camp with him. Perhaps, keep her for himself.

Nodding, the decision made, he would definitely keep her for himself.

Standing Deer hadn't felt this kind of desire for a woman for too long a time. His body was starting to react to the beauty before him. Closing his eyes for a brief second, he fought to gain control of his lustful thoughts. Was that lust he saw in her eyes, too? The Great Spirit has brought him a jewel from the skies of the Pawnee country.

Scrutinizing him just as he was eyeing her with caution and intrigue, Karen could practically read all of the thoughts as they danced across his face. Her eyes left a languorous trail of desire. He was indeed a very good-looking man, built like a god. It had been quite a long time since she looked at a man that actually interested her at all. To look at a man and feel the pulse quicken and her heart pound in her chest was an unusual reaction for her. She could sense his animal magnetism. The strong sexual attraction was glaring, forcing her to curb the desire of wanting to walk over to him, draw her hand down his chest, and work her fingers down over his taunt muscles.

He was tall, at least six feet in height, with a massive, muscular body, tanned to a golden brown. His facial features were rugged and well-defined with dark, charcoal eyes that didn't waver. He had the look of an eagle when it's hunting a prey.

He wasn't moving. Every muscle she could see was flexed, waiting for action as she imagined a warrior would. Karen could see the ripples of the muscles throughout his entire body. She wanted to touch him, caress him, and feel the hardness of his legs, arms, and chest underneath her fingertips and lips.

Karen's dream spiraled her into the mid 1800's by the mystical antique four-poster bed; offered her this man, a warrior, and her rendition of Apollo. There was no harm in following through with this uncharacteristic fantasy of hers. Licking her lips, she envisioned herself stroking him gently but firmly. She could feel his strength in her hands, going through her own body, down into her unreachable soul. How good it would feel to be his woman and have him desire her as much as she did him. Caressing that strong, massive body, while he was gently touching and stroking her most intimate places, making her tremble and quiver like no other man could. She stroked his long black hair as it was falling onto her chest as he laid her onto the ground. His shiny beautiful and thick hair was enough to make any woman jealous. She could feel his hair tickling her chest as she entwined her fingers through it in ecstasy.

Shaking her head, she blinked away the lascivious thoughts, such wonderful feelings. It obviously has been too long since she had been with a man. What a dream, too bad it wasn't real!

The sun was beating relentlessly off her back and she was sweating. Maybe, she had the temperature of the air-conditioner on the wrong setting.

Odd, does that happen in dreams? Karen felt a breeze gently blowing and pushed her bangs out of her eyes.

Uncomfortable with the journey her mind was taking, she was the first to look away. Looking around at the unfamiliar landscape was a welcome distraction. From where she was standing, Karen could hear a river somewhere nearby but couldn't see it. She watched the slight wind touch and tickle the leaves. The trees must be cottonwood or aspen. Horticulture wasn't one of the subjects she had bothered to learn. She didn't have much knowledge about different trees and plants and couldn't recall ever seeing this kind in Florida before.

Clearing her throat, Karen surveyed the campsite, avoiding the Indian's eyes. It had been a while since she had gone camping. She noted the absence of camping gear, tent, propane or gas lamps, or any equipment. In comparison to the way it appeared that this Indian lived, she was a bit spoiled.

Feeling uncomfortable under his penetrating gaze, she realized he was staring at her legs, a perplexed look on his face. His head was slightly tilted, eyes squinting as if he was trying to understand a complicated problem. Her brown silk shorts were a bit shorter than she usually wore but they were comfortable to sleep in when she wanted to take a midday nap. Her attire wasn't that unusual. Why did he look so puzzled? This Indian was reacting as if he had landed in an episode of Twilight Zone. It was only a dream, her imaginative mind running wild.

Standing Deer had finally gotten control of his senses and began to speak to her in a deep, rhythmic voice. It seemed almost hushed, as if he didn't want to break the spell. The strength of his personality projected in the sound of his voice. She couldn't understand the foreign words he spoke. He must be speaking a form of Indian dialect. How could she be dreaming and hearing a language she had never heard before? Why wasn't he speaking English?

He motioned for Karen to sit. Her legs were getting a little shaky and unsteady, she gratefully sat beside him. He offered her a piece of homemade jerky. She wasn't hungry, just curious. Surprisingly, it didn't taste that bad. Not quite like the ones you can buy at the grocery store.

Assuming he didn't speak English, she believed they needed to find a way to communicate. Sign language was considered universal. If he understood her, they would be able to continue a conversation. Karen had been learning to sign for about a year. She hoped that although she didn't have much knowledge of sign language it could be enough. Well, she might know enough to keep some conversation going, even if he signed differently than she had learned.

"Where am I?" She signed and spoke at the same time.

"Here." The Indian pointed to the ground.

"Oh, well thank you." Amused at his sense of humor, a smile tickled the edges on her mouth. "Good thing you were here, I wouldn't have been able to figure that one out without your help. Where is here?"

"This is the land of the *Scili.*" He spoke in his language and signed.

Baffled by the strange sign she inquired, "What is *Scili*?"

"Pawnee." Standing Deer said in English with exasperation.

"Are you Pawnee?" She shivered out of fear and hoped he wasn't. Though she felt compassion for the demise of the Native American cultures and people, she didn't have much knowledge of their tribes except from novels or television. She had read stories about the Pawnee and was worried, even though this was a dream. Karen certainly didn't want it to turn out to be a nightmare.

Standing Deer laughed and smiled at her. It was a refreshing and pleasant laugh, a deep and honest one. Still, the laugh didn't relinquish her fear that he may be Pawnee. She waited for his response in complete silence.

"No. I am not Pawnee. I'm Hunkpapa, from the Lakota Sioux." Unmistakable pride resounded in his voice.

It dawned on Karen that he had spoken English and had spoken it quite well. She was trying to communicate in sign language when he could speak English. Why he didn't respond to her in English before instead of hiding his knowledge of the language?

Why was she taking this dream so literally? Was her imagination playing tricks on her? She shouldn't have to keep reminding herself that it was just a dream.

"You speak English. Why didn't you speak English earlier? How did you learn?"

She scolded herself. Of course, he speaks English. How can a person have a dream and talk to someone without speaking the same language? He knows English because this was America.

It was normal for dreams to have twists and quirks that sometimes never made sense. She needed to understand that she couldn't take this as normal everyday life. Dreams weaved intricate symbolism from the subconscious mind.

"There have been white men here for a long time. I learned." He shrugged. He was blunt, short, and direct in his answers, an admirable quality. No games were involved.

"I'm Karen."

"Standing Deer."

"Well, hello Standing Deer. It is nice to meet you." Karen said formally with a slight grin on her face, putting her hand out to shake his. This dream could last a while or it could pass by in seconds. Maybe it would turn out to be a really delightful dream.

Standing Deer gently touched her hand. It puzzled her that he didn't shake it. Maybe it was a custom to greet people that way in his tribe.

She could still feel the lingering spark when she spotted a bow and arrow that was leaning beside Standing Deer. She reached over to point to it and before she could react, he grabbed her wrist, twisted her around, and had her face down on the ground.

A few colorful metaphors flew from her lips as she scrambled up and away from him. It was obvious Standing Deer had let her go, her strength was no comparison against his. Rubbing her wrist, Karen wasn't sure if she should feel angry or relieved. If he had wanted to prove his manhood, she would still be on the ground with a mouthful of dirt.

She had started to tremble with anger, frustration, and humiliation. He had her on the ground before she even realized he had grabbed her.

Note to self: take self-defense courses.

She responded to his menacing glare cautiously. Explaining her intrigue with the bow and arrow would take some time. Archery had been a sport she had been interested in learning. Karen always had an unquenchable desire for knowledge. She would like to learn to survive in the wilderness.

"I only wanted to ask you if you would show me how to make one of those and teach me how to shoot. I've always wanted to learn how to survive in the wilderness, like they did before the country became obsessed with technology. I'll need to learn how to use one if I'm going to continue to be here. Please, show me, I learn fast."

Why would she need to learn? Want, yes, need no. It was only a dream.

"Yes, I'm sure there is a lot I could teach you and I would make you a very willing student." Standing Deer chuckled, a deep-throated chuckle. The sexual undertone was rather blatant and lustful. The desire she heard in his voice was unmistakable.

It was a typical male response. Karen squirmed, uncomfortable with that type of banter. She was used to being treated by men on a professional level. As far as she knew, none of her colleagues looked at her as anything but another professional.

"I'm serious."

Standing Deer grinned enjoying her discomfort. "You don't need to learn. You are coming with me. It is too dangerous here in the land of the Pawnee. And it is even more dangerous for a white woman who doesn't know how to survive in this land." He stared at her legs. "Or wear the appropriate clothing."

Karen's mouth dropped in astonishment and then quickly closed it in anger at his arrogance. Reprimanding her for the clothes she was wearing, how dare he? It wasn't as if she planned to come here. Besides, she should be able to wear anything she wanted!

Standing Deer meant every word he said. It was a statement. It was a command and it was a fact. As far as he was concerned, nothing was going to change the fact that she was going with him. He prepared to leave. Karen cautiously watched him as he packed his gear. When he finished, he walked over to her, picked her up, and proceeded to carry her to his horse.

She inhaled deeply. He smelled of horses, leather, and his breath of recently chewed mint tickled her nose. Enveloped by how intoxicating he was, she could feel the steel strength of Standing Deer's strong and massive body as he was carrying her in his arms. Her body stirred with desire. The touch was electrifying.

It was so very pleasurable to be in his arms...

Reality hit Karen on the backside when Standing Deer plopped her on his horse. Fear gripped her while self-preservation took control. He didn't look very civilized. What if he was a savage? It was obvious his bow and arrows were not used for entertainment. What normal man would be dressed in the costume of an Indian, living off the land and riding around on his horse like it was the 1800's? This isn't going to happen, she thought. He isn't taking me anywhere. This will not turn into a nightmare.

Karen started to get off the horse when he grabbed her waist. Struggling with her to stay still, he pulled himself up behind her. She closed her eyes when he managed to subdue her without much of a struggle.

She didn't intend to be taken anywhere by some savage and uncivilized man, dressed as an Indian, and was stuck in his warped world of living alone without civilization. The dream was going all fine and dandy before he pulled this stunt.

She wished she were somewhere else, anywhere but here.

Stunned and confused, Karen found herself standing in front of the most breathtaking, beautiful waterfall she had ever seen. A glorious rainbow reflected off the mist. She never realized she had such an explicit and vivid imagination. Her dream had taken her to a paradise away from the threat of the menacing Indian called Standing Deer. She was alone.

Where was he? How did she get here? The change in location was typical of a dream, reassuring her. This wasn't Florida, not with those hills and that waterfall. In every direction, Karen could see dark, almost black hills and lush full, majestic trees. Twenty-five feet from the waterfall, she saw a cave opening. She would have to explore it.

She wandered over to the edge, fascinated by the flickering sparks from the hot sun as it beat down on the water. The pond of shimmering clear water beckoned her. Knowing she was going to enjoy the cool fresh water against her skin, she was going to succumb to its call.

Since this was a dream, she rationalized, no one would know. There wasn't a moment's hesitation. Stripping off her clothes, she jumped into the refreshing cool water. She could never have skinny-dipped when she was awake, but in this dream, it felt natural. Karen knew she was much too inhibited to do anything like this in real life.

An exhibitionist she will never be, even though she may not remember her dreams; it felt delightfully wicked. At home, she was afraid to swim in any of the ponds or lakes. She was terrified of alligators and water moccasins.

Nobody but you knows what happens in dreams unless you chose to tell someone. There was no one to judge you or chastise you. If only she could relax like this at home, Karen felt all the stress of the past few years float out of her. Now that she had her surgical license, she can finally find a position in a hospital, and have her own office in the future. Karen would be able to help those who couldn't afford an expensive doctor. She was going to make a difference.

Looking at her body, she scrutinized it as she was floating around the cool water. She looked good now and there was a sense of personal satisfaction. A year ago, she had taken a long look at herself and decided that things were going to change. She wasn't going to be a frumpy person ever again, and wasn't going to allow men to control her anymore either. She had quit smoking, lost thirty pounds, started working out on a daily basis, and liked looking at the muscular cuts in her arms and legs. Proof of the hard work she had put into her body, improved considerably by the bike riding she had started on a regular basis.

Karen hated running, bouncing around all over the place, and listening to the catcalls and obnoxious remarks from men driving by in their cars. A person could cover more territory on a bike. For someone who, a year ago, had little self-esteem as a woman, she had come a long way. Always the brain, she contemplated, never a desirable woman.

"Well, I changed that. Didn't I?" Karen said aloud. Well, almost, she pondered and smiled, knowing she still had a long way to go to build up her confidence and self-esteem. She was fine when it came to her career and everyday life but when it came to relationships, forget it. Total disasters, she just let them walk all over her.

She changed that when she broke off with David. That was her first step, getting rid of David, the one destroying her self-esteem. She could look back objectively now and see a trend. She would become involved with men she thought were strong like her father, but found they had felt intimidated by her intelligence and would hurt her emotionally just to prove their manhood.

Karen caught some movement out of the corner of her eye. She groaned, knowing the peace she had been feeling was over. Starting back to where she had dropped her clothes, she warily watched the figure come out of the trees. There was blood all over the man's chest. She swam quickly to the shore. As she was running to her clothes, the man collapsed onto the ground. His horse stood close by, guarding him. There was a considerable amount of blood on the horse, as well.

Karen pulled on her shorts, grabbed her T-shirt, and sprinted to the injured man. When she reached him, she skidded to a halt. He pulled a knife on her with a viciousness and speed that she couldn't perceive from someone who was as injured as he appeared. Shocked, she realized the man behind the knife was another Indian.

"Put that away," Karen gasped for breath. "I'm here to help you."

What is it with Indians all of a sudden? She had never had dreams about them before. Maybe, this dream was trying to tell her something.

Karen scanned the area quickly and spotted the mouth of the cave. Hoping he would understand her, she explained the necessity of needing to move him to a better place. Helping him onto his feet, together they made it to the interior of the cave. Once there, he collapsed again. Before he passed out, he grabbed her arm and mumbled in a foreign tongue.

"*Tashunca.*" My horse.

She had no idea what the Indian had said. The only thing on her mind was to attend to the injured man. She hurried outside to the sparking cool pond of water that she had just so thoroughly enjoyed, and again, taken off her shirt. This time, she planned to use it to clean the Indian's wounds. She plunged it in the water. As she was running back to the cave, Karen wished she had him in a proper facility with electricity with medical supplies. She closed her eyes and wished for anything modern and everything she could possibly need to attend to his injuries and care for him.

As she entered the cave, Karen saw that what she had wished for was right before her eyes. Stunned, she dropped the shirt on the floor of the cave. It was a huge room, completely modern, with the Indian lying on a bed beneath crisp white sheets. Delight brightened her features. Dreams were definitely wonderful, even if they were unpredictable. Too bad real life couldn't be this way.

Picking up the shirt and draped it on the back of a chair to dry.

With meticulous precision, she cleaned and bandaged the Indian's wounds. Two were very deep, long lacerations. She had sewn them quickly and skillfully.

After she completed her task and made him comfortable, Karen wrapped a towel around herself and went outside to check on the man's horse. Tying the horse to a nearby tree so it would be in the cool shade, she evaluated the horse's wounds. They were minor and she nursed them easily. Most of the blood belonged to the Indian. She believed the horse would be safe and comfortable in the shade of the trees.

She returned to the cave and saw that her Indian had awakened. He was pale from the loss of blood and she knew he was in much pain, although he attempted not to show it.

"I'm a doctor." She explained, hoping he understood her. Smiling, with her best bedside manner, she assured him to ease his fears. "I can help you. You are seriously injured and must rest."

She was gentle as she lifted his head to help him drink some water. He whispered in his language and when he realized she didn't understand him, he spoke in broken English. Moving his hands to point to himself, his voice cracked so badly that she could barely understand him. "Jumping Bull."

Tapping her chest, "Karen."

Nodding, he closed his eyes. He was weak from the loss of blood and would be sleeping soon. The medication she gave him would help him relax and get the needed rest.

Karen sat down in the chair next to the bed. Jumping Bull wouldn't be moving for a while. It will be a long wait unless, of course, her dream decided to take her somewhere else. She loosened the towel so it rested across her chest; a rest is what she needed. Dreams can be exhausting. At least, this one was. There were too many questions. Why was she dreaming of Indians? There had to be a meaning to what was happening.

Maybe she had been idle too long. Disregarding that thought, after all the schooling she'd been through, she needed the break. Her mind was trying to tell her something.

Karen woke up with a chill. As she rolled over, with her eyes still closed, she thought about the odd dream she had just had. As she lay there waiting for the grogginess to go way, she realized her hair was wet.

Wet? She bolted up and looked down at herself. She didn't have her shirt on! Dazed from her sleep, she felt the towel slip off onto the bed next to her. She stared at it, shaken and speechless. Karen leaned over the sides of the bed in search of her shirt. Not there! Reaching down, she pulled up the dust ruffle and looked under the bed. It was nowhere in sight. Jumping out of bed, she threw on another top, grabbed a dry towel, and wrapped it around her hair. What if maybe, just maybe, she had taken a shower in her sleep? She had never walked in her sleep before, but one never knows.

Heart thumping, Karen looked in the bathroom for her shirt and then continued to search the rest of the house. She couldn't find the T-shirt anywhere.

It was as if it never existed.

Chapter Two

Confounded, she sat on the bed fingering the towel, a towel that existed in her dream and should never have been in her home. It was all so extremely peculiar. The breeze in her hair, the sun pounding on her back and the tingling sensation she had felt in Standing Deer's arms. The electricity she had felt reeling through her being engulfed her. Everything had seemed so real, but it was only a dream. Wasn't it?

Of all the strangest things to experience … waking without her shirt on, and then she couldn't find it anywhere in the house. How did her hair get wet? Why was she dreaming about Indians? How can anyone dream something that turned out to be so realistic? She had never experienced anything quite like it. Thank God, she wasn't in Salem during the witch hunting years. She would be burned at the stakes.

The T-shirt had just disappeared as if it was really left behind with the injured Indian. Karen shook her head thinking everything was so odd. There had to be a reasonable explanation. Someone somewhere had to know something. But whom could she tell? Whom could she trust? Who would believe her? It was such a strange situation.

Karen couldn't shake the dream from her mind, nor her warrior, Standing Deer, stoic and proud, his strong with prominent cheekbones, and his lean muscular body. Recalling scars on his chest, she wondered where he had gotten them, how he had gotten them. What kind of battles had he been in to obtain such odd wounds?

There was absolutely not one ounce of fat on the man. She was lusting after him even now. Rubbing her hands across her face, she scolded herself. Get a grip. It was a dream, stick to reality. This man was built so well because he was a dream, a warrior to have fantasies over.

She was having a battle of wits with herself, so unusual and out of character. It's not as if she didn't know the difference between reality and dreams.

Where did that shirt go?

Puzzled and curious about her experience, Karen decided to do some research into these extraordinary dreams involving Indians. The Internet would be an excellent source to start.

Knowledge had always been a major thirst for her. Karen decided to start her research with the Sioux Indian tribe. Walking into the den, the answering machine distracted her, flashing several times alerting her to missed messages. Odd, she usually woke up when the telephone rang. She must have really been in a deep sleep. But then, if she was in such a deep sleep, how could she remember the dream so vividly, as if it happened yesterday.

As Karen was listening to the messages and jotting down whom she needed to call, she heard an unfamiliar voice. It was the woman she had bought the bed from at the estate sale. She had forgotten to give Karen the canopy that came with the bed. If Karen was interested in having it, to please call her so they could make arrangements. Karen returned her call immediately and made plans to pick up the canopy the next morning.

Settling herself in front of the computer for a complete search through the Internet, she found there was information on every tribe one could wish for, and a multitude of sites just on the Lakotas with more than enough information available to absorb. They were quite an interesting tribe. She saved site after site in her favorite places.

Intent on her reading, she didn't hear the phone ring. Hearing her girlfriend Bonnie's voice talking on the machine, she grabbed the telephone before she could hang up. Confirming their plans for dinner, Karen decided to wait to tell Bonnie about her unusual dream. Bonnie was into anything that wasn't the norm; maybe she had some ideas why Karen had this weird and unusual dream. She could interpret what it meant. However, how would she react to it?

Preparing herself for dinner, she felt as she was just going through the motions, as if she wasn't supposed to be there. She felt removed from the real world as her mind kept returning to the memory of Standing Deer and Jumping Bull. For some reason, Karen felt there was a connection between them and couldn't understand why or how. Bonnie always said she had psychic abilities but Karen never took it seriously. She just believed she had good instincts, good intuition. Why couldn't she shake the idea that there was more to this than meets the eye? There had to be answers somewhere. She decided to swing by the library before she met Bonnie at the restaurant.

At the library, Karen found a wealth of information about the Sioux Indians. She decided to concentrate on the Lakota Tribe. She could return and read up on the Pawnee and the other tribes later. As she was leaving the library, Karen made a quick about-face and picked up a couple of books on self-defense. Now, she would be prepared. She was ready to learn what was going through her mind about Indians.

Looking at her watch, she realized she was running late. Bonnie was never on time for anything but work, but she would be irritated with her tardiness anyway. She would definitely understand when she heard about Karen's unusual dream.

Interested wasn't the word. Every few minutes, Bonnie would get so excited about the dream that she would interrupt Karen with questions. The whole night revolved around discussing Karen's dream. Even at the bar when they were shooting pool, she kept questioning her about the dream.

Bonnie believed there was a very definite message. There were Indian spirits coming to Karen in her dream to let her know that she was to go and live near an Indian reservation and be a doctor for them. The dream was God's way of telling her what road she needed to travel. Bonnie was so genuinely excited about the revelation that Karen just didn't have the heart to disagree. Besides, what else could it be?

She wasn't sure about Indian spirits coming to her in her dreams. This wasn't a script from a movie: the extraordinary imaginations of writers. Spirits didn't visit you in dreams, did they? Bonnie knew she wanted to help people who couldn't afford proper medical treatment. Could this dream really be a guide to where her future lies? Dreams can tell you many things if you know how to interpret them.

Thoroughly exhausted, she arrived home just as determined as ever to learn about the Lakota Indians. What if Bonnie was right and Indians had special powers, powers given by God to reach her in her dreams. She wanted to find out as much as she could about the rituals and customs of the Indians. What if Bonnie was right?

Karen was impressed with the spiritual beliefs of the Indians and how much they depended on their religious ceremonies. She had always considered them pagans.

Pagans! They were called savages. Yet, many of their beliefs were comparable to the Christian religions of today. It was almost as if the Great Spirit might well have been called God. Is that blasphemous? Should she even compare the religions? What would it be like to watch the Sun Dance ceremony?

The Lakotas had been naturalists, still are, for that matter, loved, and respected the earth, and all its beings. They treated all life with a respect that is rare in modern civilization. They took only what they needed and left the rest to thrive and grow. The Lakota studied the trees, the plants, and animals. Those were their lessons as they grew. They were taught to be reserved and it was a necessity to possess self-control to be a good Indian. That was why Standing Deer hadn't said anything to her right away. He had been waiting to see what she was going to do or say.

Continuing her reading, she discovered that Sitting Bull was a Lakota, a chief, and a very prominent one. *Tatanka Yotanka* was his Indian name. *Tatanka* was one of the words Jumping Bull had spoken. It must mean bull. She tried to recall other parts of his name but couldn't remember. As it was, she could just barely understand him.

Karen was becoming tired and her eyes were starting to blur from so much reading. Deciding to call it a night, she slipped on her white lace nightgown, closed the books, and left them next to her on the bed. The last thing she thought of as she lay back on her pillow was Jumping Bull. Was he the same man she had read about in the research books?

Karen had just dozed off when she heard a noise. Bolting upright, she looked around at the unfamiliar surroundings. She had returned to the dark and cool cave from her dream.

Jumping Bull was moaning and restlessly moving about the bed. Walking over to him, perplexed and concerned, she thought she knew what the dream meant, that she wouldn't have another one. Maybe there was something else to this dream besides letting her know she was to serve as a doctor on a reservation.

He felt very hot and she suspected that he had a high fever. Putting a thermometer in his mouth, she checked his pulse and blood pressure.

Puzzled, Karen checked his wounds and didn't see any signs of infections anywhere. She went to the corner and grabbed a bucket to get some water. His temperature was 104 degrees. She would bathe him with the cool water from the pond. She had to break it fast. As far as Karen knew, he had never taken any kind of modern medication before and she didn't want any adverse reactions. She didn't question how the bucket got there. She just knew it would be there because she needed it. She was becoming used to having whatever she needed, at least in her dreams.

As she was bathing Jumping Bull, she put an antibiotic medication on his wounds. Karen decided to wet his hair down so she leaned him against her shoulder. She could feel his clammy skin through the thin material of her nightgown. She was soaking down his hair on his neck when Jumping Bull yelled in pain. Taking a closer look at the back of his head, near his hairline was a puncture wound, a hole festering away, just having a blast because of her neglect, its own private party. She admonished herself, feeling frustrated and disgusted because she missed it. If she had found it earlier, it probably wouldn't have become infected. She cleansed the wound, put a topical antibiotic on it, and prayed that whatever injured him wasn't poisonous. Karen had read that sometimes Indians poisoned their arrows. She prayed this wasn't the case.

Jumping Bull was resting easier and Karen decided to go outside the cave for some fresh air. She was hungry. She would search for some berries or something to eat.

Walking around, she could feel a soft breeze billowing through her nightgown. The day was hot but it was pleasant, similar to a Florida spring day. Karen felt so much peace in these hills. It was her own private little world.

She could understand why the Indians felt the way they did about their land. She decided she was going to leave Florida, find this place, and live here. It had to exist. It just had to. Now the question was, how was she to find out where she was? If she kept forcing herself to keep thinking of Jumping Bull, she would keep dreaming about him and ultimately he could tell her where she was. There was something to what Bonnie was talking about after all.

Jumping Bull's horse neighed as she approached the entrance to the cave. She had forgotten about the poor animal. It was probably hungry and thirsty. She had left the animal tied up just a few feet from the water. How cruel and unthinking can a person get?

Karen hurried over to the horse and found that it was fine. Not great, but it was doing fine. Relieved she untied the horse and watched it walk straight to the water. Good, now the horse could at least get what it needed. Unlike herself, the horse would know what to eat. She doubted very much that the horse would go far. Karen believed that horse knew exactly where her master was.

Karen climbed along the cliff, next to the waterfall, and sat down on a rock. She laid back, soaking up the sun. She could feel the spray of the water from the falls tickling her skin. She could stay here forever, never wake up, and stay in this fantasyland. No one but Bonnie would miss her. Other people would wonder what had become of her, but she doubted they would miss her.

She smiled. Now, if Standing Deer would appear, she could have a bit of sexual excitement and really enjoy herself. Karen closed her eyes and pictured the two of them entwined in a deep embrace under the waterfall. One does get an over-active imagination here, silly girl.

With a wide grin she stood and gave herself a big stretch. Sparked by her never-ending curiosity, she looked behind the waterfall and discovered an opening. Time to explore. There wasn't much space to get inside but it appeared to go further than she could see.

She couldn't go too far into the cave without a flashlight. She had done enough cave exploring to know she'd only be able to go a few feet. As she walked cautiously on the slippery and wet ground, she waited for her eyes to become accustomed to the darkness. Karen felt the smooth wet walls with her fingertips. Only a few feet from the cavern opening, she could hear the muffled sounds of the falls. The cool damp air gripped her moistened skin, her nightgown clung to her smooth, soft body causing goose bumps to crawl up her arms and legs. Satisfying unquenchable curiosity was much more appealing to her than having the chills. As her eyes became adjusted to the dark, she could see two different pathways.

A mysterious darkness encircled her. She felt as if she was intruding on sacred ground. Karen stayed to her right as she walked slowly and cautiously through the cavern. She was extremely careful, not wanting to slip and fall.

When it was too dark to see anything, she turned around and entered the main cavern. Carefully Karen explored the second pathway. She was so engrossed in the mysterious unknown of the cavern that the world outside was nonexistent. She didn't see the Indians tracking and scanning the area. She didn't know that members of the Lakota tribe were looking for their chief, Jumping Bull.

The Indians found Jumping Bull's horse and continued to search the area for their chief. They believed the chief must be nearby, otherwise the horse would have tried to make it back to the village.

The Indian warriors saw the footprints on the ground but they were scattered and kicked around. The warriors were discouraged. The sizes of the prints were that of a woman or child but the ground didn't offer the means to interpret direction. Standing Deer thought he recognized the prints, but was unsure because the ground was so difficult to read. He suspected they were the prints of the white woman he had encountered. It didn't make sense. She was days away.

They didn't see an opening to a cave. It was hidden, concealed by the powers unknown to man. Karen didn't know that she was the only one who could see the entrance and release Jumping Bull from the confines of the cave. There wasn't access for anyone to enter or exit unless she was there with them. Karen was the key.

The Indians had been gone for a while when Karen came out from behind the waterfalls. She had found a few bones but it appeared no one had been in the cavern for a long time.

She hadn't any concept of the time she had been inside. As she climbed down from the rocks, she realized the sun was close to setting. When she walked toward the entrance to the cave where Jumping Bull was resting, the horse wasn't in sight. She figured the horse could probably take better care of itself in this rugged, savage land than she could. For some reason, she knew the horse was safe and would return to her master.

Hungrier after her lengthy exploration, Karen searched through Jumping Bull's bags, hoping to find something to eat. Her stomach growled louder than Jumping Bull's snoring. She dug a little deeper and found some dried fruit and jerky.

As she munched on those, she went to Jumping Bull to check on his bandages and fever, cleansed his wounds, and applied antibiotic cream on them. His fever was down but not gone. Karen was very worried that the knife or arrow had been poisoned. Jumping Bull should have been recovering a little faster. Not wanting his death on her hands, she was determined to heal this man.

If he was hit with a poisoned arrow or knife, she should have enough medical knowledge to get him through this. Just what kind of poison did Indians use? How could she heal him if she didn't know how to treat him? How would she know if she had to use penicillin or administer some other form of anti-toxin?

Karen was tired and ready for sleep. She knew she would be going back home, ending this dream and returning to her own bed. She would be able to research what the Indians used for poison. If her strange dream continued as it was, she would be able to return and help Jumping Bull.

She closed her eyes, picturing the beauty and magnificence of everything she had seen. As she dozed, inner peace surrounded her, warming her like a favorite blanket. Karen couldn't recall the last time she had felt so serene.

Chapter Three

More refreshed than she had in years and unlike most mornings, Karen didn't walk blindly to the coffeepot for her morning caffeine boost. She didn't need a cup of coffee but out of habit, had a couple of cups anyway. The first thing she did after she poured her second cup was to eat a feast. Starving, she had cooked herself up a couple of eggs and sausage and was now popping a couple of biscuits and sweet rolls in the microwave. She needed to watch out. She didn't want to gain any of her weight back.

The telephone rang and of course, it was Bonnie. She started babbling and running on about the dream Karen had the day before. When she finally had a chance to stop her motor-mouth friend, she let Bonnie know she had another amazing dream.

She insisted on hearing about the new dream. Karen repeated everything she could recall and realized that she wasn't feeling as if it was a dream anymore. It felt more and more to her that it was really happening.

Throughout the whole conversation, Bonnie was silent. That made Karen even more wary. Something wasn't right. After she finished telling about her dream, she had to prod Bonnie into saying something, all the more scary in Karen's opinion. All Bonnie said was that she had to look into it. She hung up the phone mumbling that she had to get to work early and left Karen feeling like she was losing her grip on reality.

Look into what? What was going on? Karen felt as if she was leading a dual life. Confused, maybe she was starting to lose it.

Would they put her away? She refused to be confined in some institution somewhere. Why was she feeling so anxious? Please not now, not after all those years of studying. Too much time, money, and energy to lose everything now, she wanted to be a doctor.

Frazzled, Karen started getting ready for her appointment to pick up the canopy. As she was preparing herself to take a shower, she sat down to clean and polish her fingernails. While she was doing her right hand she stopped short.

Hyperventilating, she stared at her fingers. There was dried blood! There was dried blood and antibiotic cream underneath her nails!

"Oh my God," her voice broke, "help me."

Why was this happening? Why was it happening to me? What was going on? What was happening?

These dreams were real. They really happened. How? There was too much to lose. How could she explain this to anyone and prove that she had a hold on to her sanity?

These Indians existed somewhere, but where and when? They couldn't be real. It was impossible. It wasn't normal. Things like this didn't happen in real life. Something was definitely going on and she needed to resolve it fast. She knew Bonnie was knowledgeable about paranormal experiences. How was she going to explain to her that it was really happening?

Driving to pick up the canopy, Karen's mind was reviewing the last two dreams. Bonnie would cover the paranormal aspect, so she needed to research anything and everything she could about the Sioux Indians. She needed to find out what type of poison their enemies used. It wasn't just to satisfy her curiosity anymore.

It wasn't just a curious dream anymore. Now the knowledge was needed to save a man's life. If Jumping Bull was poisoned, she had to help him. There was a reason why she was caught in this other world or dimension. Jumping Bull was it. Why else was she chosen to go to this unknown land and have this paranormal experience? She had to save Jumping Bull for some reason and when she did, the dreams would be gone.

Jumping Bull must be a descendant of the Jumping Bull in history, Sitting Bull's father. Why was she needed? She was sure there were plenty of Native Americans who were qualified to help him. Why did these spirits, as Bonnie referred to them, come to her? She didn't know anything about the Native American people. Of course she knew about what happened in history but not of the people, nations, or traditions.

If she was going back, she needed to study on some self-defense courses. There wasn't any way of knowing how long this paranormal experience was going to continue. How would she know what kind of dangerous predicament she could get into by being in such a wild and uncivilized land? What if she was interrupting some kind of ritual or ceremony? She doubted they would accept her explanations. "Oh, sorry. I was just sent here by my dream spirits." They'd have her confined in a mental institution.

She was so absorbed in her thoughts that Karen had arrived at the woman's home without realizing it. A tall dark-haired woman answered and let her in. Karen was brought to a side porch area. The tall woman left them alone.

The woman she bought the bed from was seated on a patio chaise lounge. She was a petite, elderly woman with a happy and peaceful look on her face. She looked comfortably dressed in a long black cotton skirt and blouse. Her snow-white hair was pinned up, fashioned in a bun, with decorative pins circled around it. They re-introduced themselves and Bea offered her some coffee. Although Karen felt she had enough coffee for the day, she welcomed the offer.

She had many questions to ask this woman. They traded the usual polite chatter and then Karen finally had the chance to question Bea about her mother's bed.

"Bea, I'd like to ask you a few questions about the bed." Karen watched Bea's startled reaction as it crossed her face but she seemed to recover quickly. In Karen's mind, Bea's change of expression couldn't be misinterpreted. She knew something.

"What would you like to know, dear?" Bea asked calmly.

"Well, you see, I've had some strange and peculiar dreams since I've bought the bed." Speaking slowly and hesitantly, she didn't want to frighten the woman. "I was wondering if possibly you or your mother may have experienced anything similar."

Bea looked at her with an expression of concern. Looking toward the gardens with a distant look, she started to recall memories from the past.

"Well, dear, I never slept in the bed. I wasn't allowed. My parents were very strict with us about going into their bedroom. We couldn't enter their room without permission. The door was always locked at night. When I was very young, my mother was classified as a schizophrenic. Her best friend turned her in to the authorities to have her confined. They said that my mother had a dual personality."

Bea paused a moment and continued slowly. "My father refused to give her the medication and she wouldn't take it. They insisted that she didn't need it. He was such a good, patient man, humoring her when she spoke of her other personality. My mother would talk about George Washington and the American Revolution as if they were actually living in that time. She would talk about all sorts of people from that time period, as if they both knew them and had just spoken to them the day before. My brother, sister, and I would eavesdrop at their bedroom door sometimes and hear the strangest conversations."

Taking a deep breath, she reached up and pushed an imaginary hair away from her face, needing the moment to gather her thoughts.

"I remember one time when my father had to rush my mother to the hospital because of a stab wound. She must have inflicted injury to herself with a knife while he was asleep. How my mother got a knife like that into the bedroom without anyone knowing, I couldn't tell you. Where she got the knife, we'll never know. None of us had ever seen it before. As I recall, we never saw it after that night either.

They kept questioning my father about the stabbing. I don't think the authorities believed my parents. It was something about the way the knife wound was inflicted. She kept telling the authorities that my father didn't do it. They were trying to deliver an important message to Washington's troops when she was stabbed. The authorities wanted to institutionalize her immediately but my father wouldn't let them take her away. My father was known and respected in the community. He must have had a lot of influence because they didn't take her away from us."

Bea inhaled a deep breath and sighed. As she continued with her memories, Karen started holding her breath. She looked down at her hands and saw how sweaty they were. A lump settled in her throat making her feel as if she was being asphyxiated.

"I remember one time, as a surprise, my father had painted the bedroom for her. He had taken the canopy out of the closet and put it up. It was the only time the canopy was ever up on the bed. That's probably why I forgot about it. Well, anyway, I remember my mother was hysterical after a few days. She kept telling him that it was the canopy. They had to take down the canopy because they had to get back." Bea inhaled a shaky breath. "That was the only time I ever heard her raise her voice. She was yelling, screaming, and crying. I remember how scared I was. I had thought my father was going to have to commit her to an institution and I would never see her again. But, she didn't go, thank God. I was so scared. I guess I learned the hard way not to eavesdrop on other people's conversations.

She was just like all the rest of the mothers of my friends. She kept the house immaculate and enjoyed watching television and reading. Mama was always involved with our school and activities when we were younger. And always there with her support when we became adults."

She shrugged. "I never quite understood her dual personality. It didn't really affect our lives. She only spoke of it with my father in their room. My father seemed to understand her. He must have known that the bed had given her inner strength. Just before he died, he had told me never put up the canopy and to sell the bed after my mother died. I don't understand why, but as you know, I followed his wish. She was such a wonderful and spirited woman. I miss her very much."

Bea wiped her eyes. "I'm sorry," she sniffled. "I miss her."

"How old was she when she passed away?"

"Oh, she lived a good long life." Bea said with a broad smile. "She was 98 years old."

"And your father? How old was he?"

"Well, dear, I have no idea." Bea frowned and shook her head. "I never knew how old my father was. Couldn't tell you what year he was born, either. We celebrated his birthday on March 16th, but he would never tell us how old he was. I always thought that to be a little odd, but I guess some people are like that."

Bea smiled. One could tell she had very happy memories of her parents.

Karen absorbed the incredible story that had an ironic similarity to her own experiences. Everything Bea had told her was swarming in her head. Her sponge-like mind soaked up the information, more than she needed or wanted to know, as far as she was concerned. She felt as if she had to get out of there, before she said something she would regret.

As if reading Karen's mind, Bea finished her coffee and walked over to a box. She motioned Karen over to the table. Pulling out a section of the canopy, Karen took a quick short breath of excitement.

Hand-embroidered appliqués of flowers covered every available piece of the soft exquisite material. The kaleidoscope of colorful flowers burst on top of each other spreading across the vast field. The cotton-like fabric was yellowing from age, increasing its beauty. Bea carefully folded the section she pulled out to fit it back into the box and handed it over Karen. The box was awkward to hold but wasn't as heavy as Karen had expected.

"Thank you for telling me about your parents. I'm sorry you had to recall such painful memories from the past. You have relieved many of my worries. I appreciate you calling me about the canopy. Most people would have just forgotten it and not bothered to call."

"I couldn't have done that, dear."

Karen started walking toward the front door. "I've bothered you long enough. I must be going. I'm glad we had this chat, and I will take excellent care of your mother's bed. By the way, would you happen to know how old it is?"

Bea shook her head. "I imagined that it is at least a couple of hundred years old but really couldn't tell you, dear. I don't know much about things like that. I couldn't even give you an educated guess."

They spoke a little longer at the door about the weather and other minor things and Karen left after thanking Bea again.

Bea turned to her sister and said, "I hope she understood our message."

"I hope you didn't tell her too much." The tall woman replied as they watched Karen leave.

Karen got into her car as quickly as possible, her head spinning. So much information and Bea had no idea how much she actually knew. Karen believed that bed had some form of mystical power to allow time-travel and transmit a type of kinetic power. Karen wondered if Bea's mother had these powers, as well. She may never have the answer to that question.

She was appalled that this woman was classified as a schizophrenic, but the father knew she wasn't. He knew what was going on. Could Bea's father have been from the past? Why were they so protective of the bed? Were they afraid that the children would be classified as schizophrenic as well? Her father had to have been from the past. Otherwise, why keep his age hidden?

Instead of answers, she had walked away with more questions. Why did Bea's parents lock the bedroom door? And what about the canopy? Why did the mother panic like that when the canopy was up? Did it stop the transport into the past? Was the bed a key to the door of the past and the canopy a lock?

Were her Jumping Bull and Standing Deer from the past as well?

It isn't necessary to study quantum physics or time-travel. It's all theories, anyway. She couldn't believe she was taking this seriously. What does anyone know about time-travel anyway? No one would believe it. They would classify anyone who claimed that they experienced time-travel as a lunatic. They would put them away, lock the door, and throw away the key. Could that happen to her?

They'd put her away if she told anyone. Fear overtook her; she could lose everything! Everything she worked so hard for. She couldn't wait to tell Bonnie what Bea had said. Bonnie would probably be the only person in the world who would believe Karen and not think she was losing her mind. She had already told Bonnie almost everything. She was the only one Karen could trust.

What was she up against?

She glanced at the canopy wondering if what Bea said was true. Did the canopy stop the time-travel, as Bea's mother believed? How did she survive living a dual life?

She wasn't feeling tired. Obviously, the time-travel didn't make you lose sleep. She could test the canopy and if it stopped her from going to the past, then, she would know that the canopy was some form of lock to prevent the time-travel. She would test the canopy after Jumping Bull was healthy again.

If the time-travel was too exhausting, she'd put up the canopy until she was ready to return.

Return to the past, if that was truly where she was going. She wanted to return. Conservative, down-to-earth Karen was looking forward to returning to the irresolute past.

Karen arrived home, checked her answering machine, and returned the necessary calls. One was to arrange an appointment for a conference with an administrator at the Regional Medical Center. It was the hospital she was hoping would respond to her inquiries.

Dual lives, it might get to be a bit too much. Bea's mother and father did. Nevertheless, look what happened to Bea's mother. She was classified as a schizophrenic. In those days, they didn't know as much about psychology, especially paranormal occurrences. Karen realized she had to be extremely careful and couldn't get too involved. What if she was caught in the past and couldn't return?

Bringing the canopy into the den, she placed it on the coffee table so she could show Bonnie. Leaving her a message, she gathered the books on the Sioux Indians and went outside to finish lunch, relax, and read on the patio. She sat herself next to the pool, while she waited impatiently for Bonnie to return her call.

Karen couldn't concentrate. Restlessly, she kept jumping up and checking the telephone to see if the ringer was on. When the telephone finally rang, it was a solicitor. Irritated by the unwanted call, she returned to reading the book.

Time seemed to be moving at a slow crawl. Finally, the telephone rang again. This time, it was Bonnie. Karen felt foolish. She couldn't stop talking. After Karen was finished rambling, Bonnie said she would be over as soon as she could. Her husband was working late and she didn't need to go straight home. Relieved that Bonnie was coming over took a big weight off her shoulders. Bonnie wouldn't think she was crazy. Karen knew she wouldn't tell a soul.

Although she hired someone to do the landscaping and yard work, Karen puttered around the back yard pulling weeds out of the garden and debris off the ground. She kept herself busy trying to get her mind settled while waiting for Bonnie's arrival, needing the reassurance that she was the rational person she believed she was.

Bonnie beeped the horn as she pulled into the driveway. Karen walked around the front and saw Bonnie bending over into her trunk trying to retrieve an armful of books. With a determined expression, she told Karen she wanted to go with her.

"What?"

"I want to go with you. The next time my husband goes hunting over the weekend, I want to go into the past with you. I want to experience this paranormal encounter. What an adventure we could have!"

"Are you nuts? An adventure?"

"No, I am not nuts," snapped Bonnie. "Just help me get these books into the house. I have a lot to show you, starting with the bed you bought at the estate sale."

Bonnie placed the books on the kitchen table and pulled out one on Christian symbols.

"What did you do? Dig out all your old college books out of the closets?"

"Yes, as a matter of fact, I did. Now, come here. Let me show you something." Bonnie walked into the bedroom and went to the headboard.

"Look at the carvings on here. Remember when we were checking them out when you first bought the bed? Well, I thought I recognized some of the carving but I wasn't sure. It had been so long since I had studied the arts.

Karen, when you started telling me about those dreams, I thought there might be a connection somewhere but I wasn't sure what it was. Your dreams didn't start until after you purchased the bed, therefore, I knew the powers from the bed were from a higher power, but I wasn't sure if it was from witchcraft or from God."

Karen's heart skipped a beat before it clenched into a hard knot. "Witchcraft? What are you talking about?"

"Just hush and listen." Bonnie opened the book containing the Christian symbols. Throughout the book, she had pieces of paper marking certain pages.

"Look, right here at the top of the headboard. See this symbol? That is the symbol of the seven gifts of the Holy Spirit. If you read right here, you'll see that each dove represent the seven gifts...wisdom, understanding, counsel, fortitude, knowledge, piety, and fear of the Lord."

"It says it's from the book of Isaiah." Karen pointed to the passage.

"Yes. 'And the Spirit of the Lord shall rest upon him, the spirit of wisdom and understanding, the spirit of counsel and might, the spirit of knowledge, and the fear of the Lord.' 11:2."

"11:2?" Karen asked.

"You should read the Bible more often Karen. Chapter 11, verse 2."

"Oh."

"Over here, it's amazing, next to the angels on the right side of the headboard, see? This carving of a ship in a circle refers to Noah. The mast symbolizes the cross of Jesus. The World Council of Churches uses this as an emblem representing the mission of the church. See the letters? OIKOUMENE, it means the entire inhabited world."

Karen nodded her head and let Bonnie continue. Karen believed in God, Jesus, and the Holy Spirit but she didn't attend church. She just tried to be the best person she could.

"Now over here, the Chi Rho is the symbol of Christ, the wreath circling it is a symbol of victory. And if you look at the angels surrounding the symbols you'll see that some are holding universally recognized symbols of Christ. Now let's go look at the footboard."

Both Karen and Bonnie sat down on the floor to see the footboard's detail. Karen pushed the bottom of the comforter off the footboard onto the bed.

"Look..."

"A pentagram! I never noticed it before." Dismay ringing in her voice, "Isn't it a symbol of Satanism?"

"Yes and no." Bonnie turned to another page and handed the book over to Karen. "Here. It would be easier if you read it yourself."

As Karen read the section Bonnie got up and retrieved another book.

"The pentagram on the bed has the star upright. This," Bonnie pointed to the other book. "The star is tilted or upside-down."

"Okay, and..." Karen inquired.

"The pentagram on your bed is used as a sign to ward off witchcraft and the Evil Eye. Some people call it Solomon's Seal or The Endless Knot. As the book says, these letters S A L V S in the points are a symbol of health."

Karen rubbed her hands over her face and sighed. What happened to her simple life?

"Also," Bonnie said, "the star can be considered as three overlapping triangles, a symbol of the Trinity."

Both stared at the bed. The silence was thick, but it was a peaceful silence. Intent on studying the intricate detail of the angels, doves, and fish, Karen's fears seemed to slowly dissipate. How talented this person was, to be able to carve everything so intricately and intertwine all the symbols. It amazed her that someone could create such a breathtaking masterpiece.

"Karen, you know the angels all represent guidance and protection. It reminds me of the Angel of God prayer. You know it...

Angel of God
My guardian dear..."

"Yes, I guess it does. But it really isn't telling me what I'm supposed to be doing. Is it?"

"Karen, you're going to be fine. Just fine! Just remember that prayer and use it." With a big smile on her face, she leaned over and gave Karen a huge hug.

"Yeah, I guess I will be. Just stick by me, Bonnie. Be there for me." Karen whispered unnecessarily. "You're the only one who can know."

Karen and Bonnie walked back into the kitchen to make some coffee for the two of them. She told Bonnie everything that had occurred during the day. After a while, she asked what was in the bag.

"Clothes."

"Clothes? Thank you, but I don't need clothes. I don't have room in the closet now."

Bonnie laughed. "You can't keep wearing those clothes you're in now. And you certainly can't wear your nightgowns."

"What in the world are you talking about?"

"Clothes! Appropriate traveling clothes, for your gorgeous Standing Deer and all the rest of the people you will meet in the past." Bonnie laughed as she pulled the clothes out of the bag. "You need clothes to wear so you can fit in. I don't think our way of dressing is appropriate for that period. Do you? Maybe," Bonnie lifted an eyebrow, "that's why Standing Deer was looking at you so strangely. The other Indian you're helping..."

"Jumping Bull."

"Jumping Bull never saw you. Not really. He just thinks your some angel that has come to save his life." Bonnie laughed and hugged her good friend. "You're a good and honest person, but an angel? Ha! Just remember, I know all your secrets."

"Ha, ha, ha. Let me see those clothes." Karen walked over, handed Bonnie a cup of coffee, and started to look over the clothes.

"Oh goodness. I'm going to have to wear these things? I'm a tomboy. Tomboys don't wear dresses. And certainly not dresses down to the floor. Can't I wear jeans?"

"Quit your whining. Think of the adventure! Think about how exciting this is going to be. I've got moccasins here, too. Two pairs, try them on … the dresses, too. I'll need to adjust them so they'll fit you right."

"For Pete's sake." Karen snapped.

"Just humor me, will you?" It was obvious that Bonnie was quite amused by the whole situation. As she watched Karen struggle into the dress, her smile couldn't get any wider.

"What period are these clothes from?"

"The sales lady said they are copies from the late 1800's. I picked them up at a second-hand store. But I think you're in a time period earlier than that."

"Why do you say that?"

"Well, you mentioned that Standing Deer was Sioux. Hoping to find other names, I looked up information on Sitting Bull because he was a famous Sioux Indian chief. When I found the information at the library, I found that his father's name was Jumping Bull. Just maybe, your Jumping Bull is one in the same."

"I found a Jumping Bull in my research as well." Putting her hand on her forehead, "Are you trying to tell me I'm in the middle of the Indian wars?"

"Karen, quit stressing. No, you aren't. What have you been researching? The wars didn't start until around the time Sitting Bull was chief." She had all a calmness that was characteristic to Karen and completely out of character for Bonnie. "We don't even know if Sitting Bull is even born yet or if this Jumping Bull is his father."

"Oh, he's born. Unless he had Sitting Bull late in life, Sitting Bull is alive and well."

Karen shared all the information that she had researched about the Lakota Indians. They knew all too well that living with the Indians would be a whole different world. Books never really prepared you for reality. She had to learn about the people and their ways.

Karen continued trying on the dresses, all the while mumbling to herself about how uncomfortable the clothes were. The time went by so fast that when they looked at the clock, it was after ten. Bonnie made a quick apologetic call to her husband and ran out of the house. Karen watched as she drove off. She smiled to herself, knowing that Bonnie's husband was used to her running late all the time.

Putting the clothes and moccasins that Bonnie had given her on the bed, she decided to take a couple of pairs of jeans with her and her hiking boots as well. Her bed was piled with clothes. Hopefully they would go with her when she fell asleep.

Bonnie was right. She couldn't continue to go into the past dressed in modern clothing. Thinking about her last trip, she remembered that she had on a thin nightgown when she was there. Karen had believed she had been dreaming. Her face flushed pink, thoroughly embarrassed that she walked around like that. Jumping Bull saw her in her nightgown!

As Karen laid her head down onto the pillow, she decided to get back up and put on one of the dresses, just in case. Restless, she picked a quaint, solid sky blue chintz. The dress had a very low, plunging, and ruffled neckline with small shoulders attached to sleeves that went to her elbow.

It had a gathered waist buttoned up the front with ruffles that started from the middle of the waist, circling down to the bottom of the dress, and then went all around the hem in triple layers. The dress seemed inappropriate for the savage west, but it was the plainest dress that Bonnie had brought her. Jeans would be better.

She walked over to the closet and retrieved her 357 from the shelf, wondering if she should bring her rifle as well but decided to wait. Karen went over to the bureau, grabbed the bullets out of her drawer, loaded the gun, and slipped it into one of the deep pockets of the dress. Then, she thanked her father silently for teaching her how to hunt at a young age. She slipped the boot moccasins on and lay down to fall asleep for her trip.

Tired, restless, and anxious, Karen got up again to pick out clothes she was going to wear for her second conference with the hospital administrator. Then, she went into the kitchen and made herself some hot chocolate, grabbed the book on self-defense, and went back to the bedroom.

Karen was only a few pages into the book, when she realized she would need to go to a class. She wrote a note to herself to register for classes tomorrow and lay down. The bed was comfortable. The last thing she recalled was that she had forgotten to thank Bonnie for all she had done.

Chapter Four

Karen awoke to the sound of movement, a stale, cool smell invaded her senses. Opening her eyes, she was relieved to see she had arrived back to the cave. Standing up and stretching she looked over at her patient.

Jumping Bull, wide-awake and sitting up in the bed, she smiled at him as she walked over to see how his wounds were healing.

Unfortunately for the very modern Karen, walking in floor length gowns and petticoats wasn't a normal everyday occurrence. Stepping on the bottom of the dress, she tripped, skidded across the room, landing face first, smack dab at the foot of the bed. She started laughing at herself as she pulled herself up off the floor of the cave. Karen wiped off the dirt from the long, flowing dress and mumbled that she had to learn to walk in the blasted things.

Looking up at Jumping Bull, she saw absolutely no expression from him whatsoever. If she had looked a little closer, she would have seen the amusement in Jumping Bull's eyes.

It was obvious she wasn't accustomed to the attire she was wearing. His eyes kept roaming to the chair, his mannerisms had a slight change in demeanor. He most likely recalled what she had been wearing before and wondered why she changed her style of clothing. Turning to look in the direction of the chair, she saw the gun and box of bullets that traveled with her. A puzzled expression fluttered across his face. She understood his confusion and curiosity. Explaining how she managed to bring the items with her, how she landed in Sioux territory without being seen by anyone was beyond her or his comprehension.

Not wanting to trip again and make a fool of herself, Karen walked the few steps around the side of the bed slowly and cautiously.

Note to self: practice walking around in dreadful, encumbering dresses and skirts.

Checking Jumping Bull, she could see there obviously had not been poison involved or he would still be very sick. He sat there, still as can be, letting her check his wounds without a word. Karen found the silence to be refreshing, especially after being with Bonnie most of the night.

She recalled a few occasions when her patients would babble from nervousness no matter how much she tried to keep them relaxed. Applying more ointment on Jumping Bull's wounds, she grabbed the thermometer from the drawer. Jumping Bull leaned back and gave Karen a wary look.

"It checks your temperature." Smiling as she nudged it under his tongue, she checked the wound at the nape of his neck. It was healing well. "Let's go outside and get you some fresh air." Smiling, she was relieved with his recovery, his natural coloring had returned.

Jumping Bull got up slowly from the bed; "I not find how to leave."

"Well, I'm glad you didn't leave until I knew you were better. The door is right there." She pointed to the right of the bed.

With eyes wide with astonishment, he looked to where she pointed. Jumping Bull had not seen the door earlier. He gave Karen a puzzled look and followed her as she exited the cave. He had gone over the whole cave and had not found one exit. The Great Spirit had brought him something indeed. How had she gotten in the cave without him seeing her enter? How did she get in? One second, his eyes were closed and no one was around and the next, he opened his eyes and she was there sitting on the chair. She must be very powerful. Maybe she was a daughter of the Great Spirit come to earth to help the Indian Nation. She had come at a good time. The ceremonies would be starting soon.

The sun was bright as they went through the cave passage to the outside. Karen reached into her pocket and put on a pair of sunglasses. She was glad she had thought of getting her gun. When she retrieved the bullets out of her bureau drawer, she grabbed her sunglasses as well.

"What those?" Jumping Bull asked as he pointed to the glasses.

"They are sunglasses. They protect your eyes." Taking them off, she handed them to him. "Do you want to try them?"

Jumping Bull twirled them around and looked at them from every angle possible. He put them on and scanned the area. With his deerskin pants and shirt, graying braided hair down to the middle of his back, and adorned with feathers, the combination looked odd.

Not any funnier than she did, looking at the dress she was wearing. None of the other clothes came with her, answering one of the many questions. In order for her to bring anything back with her; she must be wearing or holding whatever she wanted to take.

Jumping Bull was looking around and surveying the area. "It makes sunshine dark. I use them, a while." He nodded his head in acknowledgment. "My horse be back. Warriors come to find me, didn't. Warriors took her with them. I go hunt something to eat."

Turning around to enter the cave to get his bow and arrow, he was startled when he didn't see the opening to the cave. "Where cave opening?"

Karen turned around and pointed to the opening. She watched Jumping Bull's eyes widen with disbelief and excitement. He took off the sunglasses and looked closer, inspecting the exterior of the cave and entrance.

"Door not there until you turn around, point to it," astonished and more convinced she had sacred powers, making things appear and disappear.

Puzzled, Karen stood at the entrance as she watched him grab his bow and arrows and walk back out of the cave. It didn't make sense. What did he mean, it wasn't there?

Jumping Bull turned around and told her he would return. Karen walked over to the pond and reflected on everything that was happening to her. The cave opened and closed to her only. How can that happen?

She could transport herself from area to area by willpower. The limitations and the possibilities could be endless! Just imagine what she could accomplish!

She decided to try something small, perhaps make the leaves and branch move on the tree nearest to her. Staring at a small section, she concentrated on moving the leaves. She couldn't tell if the leaves moved because of the wind. Concentrating harder, she focused on shaking the branch. After a few moments the leaves moved and the branch began to shake.

A branch was on the ground approximately ten feet from the edge of the pond, she attempted to lift the branch off the ground. She didn't hear the three Indians approach on their horses.

The Indians paused to watch this strange white woman staring at the ground as if she was possessed. Talking among themselves quietly, they wondered what she was doing. Before approaching her, they looked around to see if anyone else was with her. They knew she couldn't possibly be alone, there had to be a white man around somewhere, and were prepared. One of the horses neighed.

Whipping around at the sound, she guiltily thrust her hands in the air. She didn't want Jumping Bull to see what she was doing. Before her sat three of the fiercest looking Indians she could imagine. There were four horses, the fourth Indian wasn't within sight. Clasping her lips firmly together, her eyes scanned the area, searching for the warrior.

The three young men, faces painted with black stripes and white circles, all had feathers in their hair. One of the warriors had earrings made of beads in both of his ears; another had a bear-claw necklace. They conversed among themselves as she stood staring at them. Were they from Jumping Bull's tribe or were they from another band? She didn't have the knowledge to tell the difference.

Discreetly, she reached into her pocket to hold onto her gun. Karen knew she had to keep it hidden from them. She wasn't sure she was in danger but something was telling her to be careful, to be extremely careful.

The Indian with the beads in his hair dismounted his horse and walked over to her. She quickly noted the knife on his belt, started to back away and was ready to run.

She turned to run when he jumped and grabbed a fist full of her hair. He swung her around, twisting her hair around his fist and arm. In the bustle, Karen had let go of the gun. He had her pressed hard against his chest and body. The more she fought and kicked, the harder he pulled on her hair. He had her bound and helpless.

The gun hidden underneath the skirt of her dress, gave her hope. She moved it between her feet, considering alternative ways out of the new predicament.

Chest heaving she forced herself to relax and as she did, so did the Indian. His lips were close to her neck and she could feel him breathing on her. He spoke quickly to the other Indians. Both men had already dismounted. The one with the Bear Claw necklace stood with his arms across his chest while the other walked over to her, wide grins on both of their faces.

Karen could feel him, hard and ready against her bottom, rubbing against her and kissing her neck. Pulling away from him, he tightened the grip on her hair. Grinning, he purred something in her ear. She may not have understood a word he spoke, but his body gave full indication of his desire.

The Indian with the earrings reached for the bodice of her dress pulling it wide open exposing her breasts. Kicking him, he jumped back to avoid her foot spotting the gun immediately and grabbed it. Karen held her breath. The Indian took the gun, rubbed it on her private parts, and then slowly rubbed the gun up her abdomen to her breasts. He encircled her breasts and then, gently and slowly, up to her neck. Before she had time to realize what was to be next, she was on the ground. Pummeling anything within her reach, she screamed, punched, and kicked. She was giving the warriors a fierce fight. Watching and laughing, the warrior with the bear-claw necklace was entertained by the scuffle and impressed by her courage.

"*Hiya!*" Jumping Bull yelled as he ran toward the group. "*Hiya.*"

"Thank God, Jumping Bull!"

Running over to the three warriors, Jumping Bull yelled to the Indians. The two men let go of her immediately. As she was scrambling to her feet, she pictured herself pulling the man with the bear-claw necklace by the hair. By sheer force of her will, he was yanked backward. Closing her eyes, she shook the vision from her mind. The Indian looked behind him, expecting to fight. Puzzled, he reached up to rub the back of his head. Covering herself with her torn dress, she buttoned what she could.

She watched as Jumping Bull spoke to the men. The Indian with the earrings reluctantly handed Karen's handgun back to her. They didn't look very pleased with whatever Jumping Bull was telling them.

Jumping Bull knew this woman was going to be an important part of his life. They were going to be lifelong friends. She had come from somewhere and the Great Spirit had brought her to him. He had informed the warriors that she was under his protection.

Speaking calmly and with respect to Jumping Bull as they walked over to their horses, she watched as the Indian with the bear-claw necklace took the rider-less horse and walked him over to where she stood.

"*Wanunhecun.*" He reached out to hand the reins to Karen. When she didn't accept the gift from the Indian, he shook the reins and repeated, "*Wanunhecun.*"

Karen looked at Jumping Bull unsure of what she should do.

He leaned toward her and spoke quietly into her ear. "They Cheyenne warriors. They not harm you again. Now, they know you friend of Jumping Bull's." He told them more than that but Karen had no idea what.

"What is '*Wanunhecun*'?"

"That Indian's way of asking forgiveness. It mean mistake. Horse peace offering, he no want bad luck to follow him. I tell them you have great medicine. Important to make peace with you or bad luck follow warriors."

"That's a terrible thing to tell him. Why in the world would you go and tell them something like that?"

"You have much power, little one. They can be used for good or bad."

Jumping Bull had been successful in his hunt for food and asked the warriors to join them. As they cut up the rabbits Jumping Bull killed, the men spoke quietly among themselves. Jumping Bull was conferring with the warrior who had the bear claw necklace. He was honored to be the warrior to have the daughter of the Great Spirit with him.

He thanked the Great Spirit for the chance to prove himself worthy. Jumping Bull would protect her, this woman Karen, as she called herself, this spirit of the mountain.

Karen was fixing her dress with the tools Jumping Bull had given her. She wished Bonnie were here to do it. Watching her fumble with the dress, she could see the twinkle of amusement in his eyes as he noticed her lack of capabilities to do womanly chores. She stitched his wounds with precision. Yet, when it came to life's minor necessities, she was unskilled.

After they finished the meal, the three warriors bid their farewells. She watched Jumping Bull and the men walk to where the horses had been tied.

She recalled Jumping Bull's words. "You have much power, little one. They can be used for good or bad." She was determined to never forget those words. It was a warning to her to be careful with what she thinks. She could seriously hurt someone if she wasn't careful.

Jumping Bull was a very wise man with a lot of spiritual and practical knowledge. It was exciting and scary to know that she had kinetic abilities, once she had control over them the possibilities were endless. This kind of power in the wrong hands would be catastrophic.

Karen pictured the headboard with the Emblem of the Seven Gifts of the Holy Spirit. It was there as a reminder, so whoever had the bed would use the powers with the Lord in mind at all times. These powers must be used with the gifts in mind, never to be abused. She was beginning to sound like Bonnie. There was something behind what Bonnie believed and she was right in the middle of it.

Karen enjoyed the silence. The peace and serenity she felt when she was in the past was a blessing. There hadn't been any major stress except for the little episode with the Cheyenne.

There wasn't a clock hovering, pushing everyone to rush here and there. At home, everywhere, people were rushing, for what, to save five minutes? Here, one just takes it as it comes.

Simplicity seemed to disappear in the modern world and the need to have all the luxury's life had to offer had taken control. Her world consisted of concrete buildings, paved streets, the biggest, the best, and the most recent technological gadget. No one was satisfied with what they had, with what life had to offer.

Even she had fallen into the trap of material things.

Buying a huge home with four bedrooms, three baths, formal living, an office, a den, a family room, and it was just for her. Why did she feel she had the need for such a large home? The tax break was nice, but she could have done something else? She could have purchased 60 acres somewhere for the same cost and had a small house built on the land. If she ever found the right man to marry, then they could add on to the house if it was needed. She shook her head, pursing her lips together, dissatisfied with herself, with the shallow attitude that she had developed.

A newer car was needed, perhaps a hybrid, especially if she acquired the job with the hospital. The new department would network with the hospital. The administrator had emphasized that she wouldn't be required to be in the office every day.

It wasn't the position she had originally applied for but she liked the idea of the traditional home visits. She would be treating people in their homes so they didn't have to go to a doctor's office, just like her father did. Her father preferred house calls. He believed it was better for the patient.

Here, it was a different world. She silently watched the warriors standing near their horses preparing to leave. If Jumping Bull would be willing to teach her everything he could, she could survive in this time period without the need of anyone else's protection. He could have someone else teach her. He may not have time for her, especially if he was chief, like Bonnie believed.

As he sat beside her, she put the sewing aside. "Jumping Bull, there is much for me to learn if I'm going to continue to stay here. I don't know how to take care of myself in this unfamiliar land. My father taught me to hunt. But I don't know how to live off the land." She looked at the clouds in exasperation and pointed to the trees and plants. "I don't know what berries or plants are edible. I don't know how to shoot a bow and arrow. Nor do I know how to throw a knife. I wouldn't survive without someone to protect me. I'm a very independent person. I don't want to have to depend on anyone else to survive, or need a protector. I want to do it myself."

Karen looked at him with hope that he would agree to help her. She waited in silence for his response.

"If what you say true, I help you. When I can. I have many good warriors and women in the village who help you. They teach you ways of land, ways of Indian. As daughter of Great Spirit, how you come this far and not been taught way to live as people do? Not my place to question Great Spirit but did you not listen to lessons? You are child of Great Spirit. Do you know why the He has brought you here to the land of the Sioux?"

Karen was puzzled by Jumping Bull's questions and unsure how to respond. She was well-educated. How could she explain her ignorance without making herself out to be an idiot; lack of knowledge that he considered mandatory for survival. Books were one thing, surviving in the wilderness another.

She spoke cautiously, unsure of his knowledge of the ways of the white man. "Where I'm from, there aren't many trees and wildlife unless they drive out to the country. Stores supply food, drink, clothing, and anything else needed. The buildings are made of concrete and steel, the streets are made of concrete as well." She reached up her arms to emphasize the height of the buildings, in comparison to the trees. "Some of the buildings are two hundred and three hundred feet high, taller than the highest tree.

One doesn't use horses for transportation, they use large vehicles on wheels, called cars or trucks. They use fuel, gasoline to make them go, and are driven on these streets, what you call trails or paths, made of concrete. There are highways and expressways so you can go fast to wherever you want to go. There are hardly any dirt roads; usually one finds them in very remote areas of the country. It is a very different world."

Karen paused to see if there was a slight change in expression, but found none. Jumping Bull would be a proficient poker player. He sat silently waiting for her to continue.

"Hunting is a sport, it is something we do for fun and enjoyment. It isn't normally a necessity to hunt for food. Even though my father taught me to eat what we hunted and not kill animals just for sport, not everyone does it that way." She touched his arm. "God, the Great Spirit teaches us humanity and has given us laws to live by. We're all children of God, of the Great Spirit. I'm a normal person, just like you. I've just been chosen to come here and live this life to the best of my ability. I've been given many great powers that I don't yet know how to control. I don't always have these powers. I have knowledge of medicine because I studied it for many years. Those are the only powers that I'm truly sure of. I can heal most people, cure some illnesses, and I do my best to try and help all people."

He listened with every sense of his being. He didn't interrupt but let her finish her thoughts. She could see many questions rushing through his mind.

Jumping Bull nodded his head to acknowledge everything she said. "I will think," not ready to ask her about her strange world. He wasn't sure if he really wanted to know.

Reaching into his bag, he handed her the sunglasses.

"Don't you like them?"

Jumping Bull grunted. "I not hunt good with them blinding my eyes. *Oiyokpasya.* It makes sun dark. My horse return soon. It is good Cheyenne give you horse. I would like you to come with me when it time to leave. There many things we teach each other." Hoping she would agree, he planned a great feast in her honor to thank her for saving his life.

Jumping Bull handed her a piece of meat and they both ate in silence.

Grabbing his bow and arrow, he stood. "Let us go." Jumping Bull said quietly.

Karen jumped up enthusiastically, grumbled as she stepped on her dress, and followed Jumping Bull. They walked beside the pond toward the woods. She was about to get her first lesson in survival.

"Don't like dress, do you?" he laughed.

Chapter Five

Standing Deer was glad he finally spoke to Sitting Bull about his dreams, hoping Sitting Bull would understand what they meant. The haunting footprints had finally brought him to Sitting Bull's lodge. He wasn't sure if they were her prints when he first saw them.

Yet, Standing Deer kept having dreams about the woman. He couldn't get her off his mind, repeatedly dreaming the whole experience every night. There was a magnetism he couldn't forget. He woke up trembling from the memory of how she had felt in his arms, longing for her. Even now, riding next to Two Feathers on their way to where they found Jumping Bull's horse, he could still feel her body against his.

He could recall the sweet smell, the soft touch of her hair, the urgent desire to want to make love to her, right then and there. Standing Deer closed his eyes slowly and seized the memory of how she had felt next to him. He took a deep breath allowing his mind to ravish itself. All sights and sounds escaped him. He could only think of the white woman, Karen.

"Standing Deer, what world are you in?"

Startled out of his memories, Standing Deer looked blankly at Two Feathers.

"I asked you if you were feeling well."

"I'm fine. Why do you ask?"

"I have never seen you behave like this. Your mind is very far away. Are you sure nothing is bothering you, my friend?"

"It's that woman." Standing Deer breathed deeply. "She will not leave my mind. I know it was her footprints. She must know what has happened to Jumping Bull. I can't explain it but I believe she will lead us to him."

Two Feathers arched one eyebrow but didn't pursue questioning Standing Deer. He knew Standing Deer's dreams had a lot to do with his behavior in the last few days. It was obvious the woman was on Standing Deer's mind and not just because of Jumping Bull. He had never seen Standing Deer act so strangely. This woman must be something if it had Standing Deer all flustered.

Two Feathers knew his friend had not been with a woman since his wife died four years ago. As far as he knew, he had not been interested in anyone. He definitely had plenty of choices among the unmarried women of the tribe. There were many that would be honored to be his wife.

Friends since boyhood, they learned together, hunted together, even did the Sun Dance together. They both had the same amount of coups until Standing Deer's wife and unborn child had died of the white man's disease.

Ever since, he worked harder and received more coups than anyone in the tribe. Everyone knew it was his way of mourning his wife and child's death. Even still, Standing Deer was highly respected among their tribe.

Two Feathers and his wife, Laughing Flower, stood by him the whole time she was sick. They would take turns feeding and caring for her. Laughing Flower did all of the work that needed to be done in Standing Deer's lodge. After his wife's death, Laughing Flower continued to help until he growled at her one morning that he wasn't a puppy and didn't need to be treated like one.

The next day, Standing Deer had left his dead wife's horse in front of their tent. Even encircled by his deep sorrow, he still had compassion in his heart.

Standing Deer was happy Sitting Bull had told him to take Two Feathers with him. They had been blood brothers since childhood. They were the best riding companions and warriors. Together, they were never defeated. Whatever Two Feathers wasn't strong at, Standing Deer was. Wherever Standing Deer wasn't strong, Two Feathers excelled.

Two Feathers had the biggest heart of gold he had ever seen in any man. As far as his friend was concerned, there was no evil in a man. He was idealistic, to a fault maybe. Though he wasn't a medicine man, he would find all sorts of injured creatures and bring them to his lodge to heal them.

Standing Deer remembered how hard it was on Two Feathers the first time he had killed a man. It was a trapper. The crazy white man had tried to kill Two Feathers and he reacted exactly the way he was taught. Survival is a strong motivator. He was taught well, the way of the Lakota warrior. It was pure instinct to slash the man's throat.

He had been shaken by it for weeks until Standing Deer, fed up with his moping around, had finally told him that it was either his death or the trapper's. Which one would Two Feathers prefer it to be?

His friend had found the perfect mate. Laughing Flower was precious. She was like a sister to him. She had a good sense of humor and a wonderful outlook on life. Her energy was abundant, like a child. Just don't get her mad or she'd kick you like one.

They had listened with undivided attention when he had told them of his experience with Karen. She had teased him, saying he had finally found someone as stubborn as he was and there would be much noise coming from his lodge once he found her again. She teased, that was, of course, if he was warrior enough to keep her in one place.

Standing Deer felt a tap on his arm. Two Feathers lifted his chin, pointing it toward a clearing where Jumping Bull and a woman were getting ready to shoot a handgun. It appeared to them that the woman was showing Jumping Bull how to use the small gun that was in his hand.

Two Feathers let go of Long Horse Hair's reins and let him run to his master, Jumping Bull. The two warriors rode their horses slowly to the clearing. Two Feathers was zealously looking over Karen. In his opinion, as far as he could see, she was everything Standing Deer had described...and more. She was beautiful. His friend couldn't have described her better. Her hair had so many colors all shimmering and radiating from the reflection of the sun encircled her and shined from her being. He smiled with complete understanding.

Standing Deer's demeanor change, sitting taller and prouder on his horse, his breath was coming faster as they got closer. His eyes didn’t leave the woman.

It was the woman for Standing Deer. The Great Spirit has indeed blessed him. He hoped the woman felt the same way about his friend.

Jumping Bull heard the hooves and looked up to see his horse trotting toward them. The reunion was a happy one for both master and his beloved animal. Not far behind the horse, Karen watched two Indians approaching them.

Was it him? She couldn't be certain with the sun shining in her eyes, couldn’t get a good glimpse of what they looked like. That stature was unmistakable. Inhaling a deep, shaky breath she felt her heart palpitate in excitement. Hope was in her heart, she wanted to see him again and feel the things she felt while she had been in his arms.

What if he was married? She hadn't thought of that before! Karen let out a heavy, defeated sigh. He had to be married. He's a grown man, about thirty years old. An extremely sexy and strong warrior like him probably had six kids running around and possibly two wives. Two wives probably wouldn't even slow him down.

What was she thinking? She couldn't fall in love with someone from the past. It would make life too complicated.

Jumping Bull heard her sigh and saw the sadness and disappointment on her face. He was puzzled by the change in her. Misunderstanding her reaction and sadness, he promptly told her she didn’t have to worry. She was safe.

Karen watched as the two Indians dismounted off their horses. Jumping Bull was greeting them. They were having a lengthy conversation. It was all in Lakota and Karen had no idea what they were saying.

It was him! His hair was braided to one side with a leather strap fastening a singular feather that lay across his chest, his copper skin glistened from the heat of the sun. He wore nothing but a loincloth.

Trying to unsuccessfully calm herself, her heart pounding, she felt like pudding. If she didn't slow her breathing down, she would hyperventilate. They would surely see her heart thumping right through the stupid dress. She couldn't understand the childish school girl reaction, her palms were sweaty, her hands shaking. No one...not one person in her whole life had ever made her react this way. Her heart was racing a mile a minute, She was more nervous than she had ever been in her lifetime.

Jumping Bull turned to Karen to introduce the men. Two Feathers nodded his head, offering her a wide smile that lit up his entire face. She liked him immediately. The man was dressed in a loincloth, with leather tied to both his lower arms, unlike Standing Deer who had only one on his left arm. She wondered if this smiling warrior was capable of shooting his bow and arrow with both hands.

Standing Deer, with a lighthearted grin, told Jumping Bull they had already met. Jumping Bull looked at Standing Deer with raised eyebrows questioning his statement, but said nothing.

Turning to Karen, Jumping Bull asked, "You have anything you want bring?"

"Yes. My medical bag is in the cave." Walking toward the cave entrance she saw the two warriors surprised reactions. Smiling, she kept walking.

The two warriors eyed each other.

Two Feathers spoke in Sioux. "What cave?"

"I will explain what I can on our way home. And you, Standing Deer, can tell me about your experience with our little one."

Two Feathers didn't know much English, putting many Lakota words in his sentences. He was curious and kept the conversation going on their ride to the village.

Feeling off balanced with Standing Deer so close to her, she couldn't help herself. Her eyes would stray and look away each time he would look in her direction. The magnetism between the two was discomforting. Was he feeling the electric pulse sparking between them or was it just her?

She would catch him grinning at her. He didn't look away, looking more amused at her avoidance than anything else.

Interrupting her thoughts, the man had the audacity to ask, "Why are you dressed like that?" He started to chuckle and caught himself before anyone could hear it.

Frowning, she thought attempting to dress like other women from this time period would help. Uncomfortable at his scrutiny, she pulled the top of the dress up where it barely covered her breasts. She wasn't accustomed to wearing this clothing.

"What was I supposed to wear?"

He winked, "What you were wearing before would be fine."

She squinted her eyes at him, "Really?"

Smiling he looked away. "Would have been easier to get on the horse."

"Hm." recalling her comical attempts to straddle the horse with the long dress catching and binding her legs, she blushed.

It took three tries to get on the horse, with the dress fighting her the whole time. Finally, she had wrapped it around her arm and jumped up exposing her muscular legs. Once she was atop the horse, she strategically tucked the dress. She had ridden for years and refused to allow a dress to defeat her. She had been determined to mount that horse on her own. Karen knew they didn't think she could ride, especially with her having so much trouble mounting the horse. She proved them wrong, riding like a seasoned horseman.

As they rode northward, the mountains to her left and the plains to her right, she relished in its breathtaking scenery. The wilderness was hostile but she was comforted knowing she was with Indians that knew how to survive in this land.

They rode until after dark, camping overnight near a river. Standing Deer gave her a blanket to lie on while she slept. As she dozed, she hoped that her leaving them wouldn't make them think she was deserting them. How would they react when they saw she was gone? She could hear the three men talking quietly around the campfire as she drifted to sleep.

Jumping Bull was the only one who wasn't startled. He smiled at the two curious warriors and explained she would return in the morning. Unruffled by Karen's disappearance, he went to sleep. Two Feathers and Standing Deer didn't say anything to each other, too startled by the sight to say anything.

Karen awoke at the campsite with the aroma of food teasing her senses. Opening her eyes slowly, she saw Standing Deer squatting near the fire, staring at her. She smiled at him satisfied with the accomplishments she had made while the three Indians slept.

It was pure luck that her new job didn't start for a month. She told the administrator she was going to take a three-week vacation and would call him when she returned. Then, she and Bonnie agreed to try out the canopy and see if it kept her in the past. Excited about the decision, she would be able to live with the Indians and experience this wilderness, undisturbed. Bonnie kept saying she was jealous and couldn't wait for hunting season to start so she could go with Karen.

Standing Deer interrupted her thoughts and asked quietly. "Where do you go?"

Karen thought out the answer very carefully. She wasn't sure how much Standing Deer would understand without it sounding like it was magic.

"I go home," Karen said slowly. "When I fall asleep here, I go to another place and when I fall asleep there, I come back here."

Standing Deer shook his head in confusion. "I don't understand."

"I don't either." Putting her hair into a ponytail, "my friend Bonnie believes, God has chosen me..." correcting herself, "the Great Spirit has chosen me to do special things. My home is far from here, where I have work to do, with many people to help. And here...there are important things that need to be done, also. But I'm not sure what the Great Spirit has in mind for me yet. I just know there is a reason why I have come to you and this land."

Hoping she had explained it without telling too much, she watched his reaction. Standing Deer nodded his head in acceptance.

When Jumping Bull and Two Feathers arrived back to the little campsite everyone ate and headed to the village. Jumping Bull told her it wouldn't be a long ride.

A few hours later, as Karen was watching the horizon, Standing Deer touched her arm and pointed northward. She couldn't see anything but the high grass billowing in the wind. As they rode closer, she concentrated on where he had pointed. The village blended into the landscape so well that she could just barely see the lodges. If a person wasn't looking or didn't know they were there, they wouldn't have seen the village, at least, not until they were right on top of it.

Excitement trickled throughout the village as they entered. One Indian yelled something to Jumping Bull, hopped on his horse and took off at a fast run. People were hustling and bustling around. With everyone talking to the three Indians all at once, there was a lot of confusion.

Three women had run up to Standing Deer. A tiny woman, with a baby in her arms, came running up to Two Feathers and gave him a huge hug. Karen could see a lot of love shared between the two of them.

Feeling forgotten and overwhelmed by all of the confusion going on around them, she felt uncomfortable, out of place. The feeling didn't last long.

An elderly woman came out of the largest lodge in the village, confident with beauty and grace. Walking to Jumping Bull, she spoke so fast Karen was surprised he could keep up with her, her voice soaked with concern. Jumping Bull turned, sweeping his open hand toward Karen and said something in Lakota to the people that had surrounded the party of travelers. Instantly there was a roar of cheer and excitement.

Standing Deer helped her off the horse and the women came up to her and gave her hugs. The men kissed her on the forehead and told her, "Wopila eciya niye." Thank you.

After the excitement died down, Jumping Bull's wife took her to their lodge. Within a few moments, another woman and Two Feather's wife came into the lodge with exquisitely decorated dresses. She openly admired the elaborate handwork, touching them and feeling a softness that she knew took hours of work to accomplish.

Looking at Jumping Bull's wife, she nodded her head. "Beautiful."

The woman made washing motions around her body and hair. Karen nodded and told them yes, desperately.

The three women escorted her to a deserted area of water, handing her some soap. They sat on the edge of the water, and chatted with each other while she bathed. The soap smelled like English lavender. The invigorating bath made her feel like a whole new person, completely refreshed from the long ride on the trail. Two Feathers' wife handed her one of the deerskin dresses and Karen put it on.

More comfortable than that long thing she had on earlier, she was relieved it went to the middle of her calf and not to the ground. At least she could walk and not worry about falling on her face. The dress was fringed around the arms and bottom of the dress. The beadwork must have taken hours, created with careful, loving hands.

Two Feathers stood outside the lodge, calling to the women to see if he could enter. When he came in he told Karen, "Good, *waste*. More better?" honoring her with his wonderful smile.

"Yes. Yes, thank you very much."

With his hands moving rapidly in Indian sign language, Two Feathers spoke slowly, "Jumping Bull *kicicopi*. *Woyuonihan* for you. Come."

Walking out, the women followed. Jumping Bull's wife grabbed Karen's arm and escorted her to the center of the village.

Standing Deer approached her, giving her a mischievous smile, "You look wonderful, Karen. Maybe someday I can see you in that strange attire again."

Blushing, Karen was brought over to be seated next to Jumping Bull who was speaking with a warrior. Karen took the time to watch everything that was going on around her. The happiness in the camp was contagious. Everyone had worked together with the preparations for the feast while she had been with Jumping Bull's wife. She felt a little bit of hostility around her, but it was expected. After all, she was a white woman.

Across the way, Standing Deer was surrounded by three women, the same women that had greeted him upon their arrival. His wives?

She had already decided falling in love with him would be a tremendous mistake, an impossibility. She couldn't live in both worlds forever, nor would it be fair to him or their children, a pointless thought since he was already married. She was determined to stay away from Standing Deer, avoiding the magnetic pull was best.

Karen saw him watching her, her silence impressing him, making it easy to teach her their ways. She didn't realize that his two sisters, Sunshine in the

Morning and Little Fox were relentlessly questioning him about the beautiful woman. They had decided Karen was perfect for him. Even their friend, Yellow Bird, was excited about the woman even though she had hoped to be his wife someday.

Karen turned her gaze away from Standing Deer and watched two Indians approaching Jumping Bull. She was surprised to see the warrior with the bear-claw necklace. What was he doing here? The other Indian was in a breechcloth and had scars on his chest just like Standing Deer. There was something different about him. He walked with a presence. She could see by the Indians; reactions in the camp that he was important. He was a good-looking man with distinguished features. The feathers in his hair fluttered as he bowed his head to Jumping Bull and spoke to him in Lakota.

The Indian with the bear-claw necklace recognized Karen immediately. She could feel his uneasiness and tension building. He didn't let anyone see it, he would do well at poker, too. Karen nodded her head to greet him when Jumping Bull introduced Karen to the two Indians.

"This warrior Sitting Bull," pointing to the Indian with the many feathers. "You meet this warrior. He Gray Eagle from the Cheyenne and honored Dog Soldier. He has honor to carry Dog Rope and great warrior among his people."

Jumping Bull paused. "Sitting Bull great warrior in his people's eyes. He has many coups and from Hunkpapa tribe." Jumping Bull paused and looked at Sitting Bull with admiration in his eyes. Turning to Karen he whispered to her, "It custom you stand to greet, honor them."

Not wanting to offend anyone, she quickly stood. She was unsure of their customs and prayed that instincts would pull her through, with a little guidance from Jumping Bull. Karen looked from one Indian to the next.

Gray Eagle touching her hand, smiled, and in the Lakota language, "*Niye wopila eciya.*" Thank you. Jumping Bull translated for her.

She returned his smile and said to Gray Eagle, "It is an honor to meet such a great and honored warrior of the people."

Aware that Gray Eagle didn't want the white woman to know he understood her language, Sitting Bull turned to Gray Eagle and translated what she had said. Gray Eagle nodded his head and walked over to the other warriors that were standing in a group watching the introductions. Karen kept silent. She wasn't sure if she was to speak first but she knew Sitting Bull had something to say to her.

After a few moments, taking her hands, Sitting Bull spoke slowly and quietly to make sure everything he said would be as accurate as possible, without any misunderstandings. "I thank you for saving Jumping Bull's life. It is an honor to meet someone with the great powers you possess. You will always be in my heart as an honored friend. It is a great deed you have done and we owe our livelihood to you. I honor you this day and make you my friend for life." Sitting Bull kissed her on the forehead.

Karen waited a few moments, instinctively mimicking Sitting Bull and the way of the people. She also spoke slowly, "It is an honor to meet the great Chief Sitting Bull. You have done many great accomplishments in the past and will continue to honor your people in the future."

Karen paused, and then continued, "I accept your friendship with honor and give you mine. I pray to the Great Spirit that I may never dishonor you or your people."

Sitting Bull waited a moment, shaking his head, "I am not chief. Jumping Bull is our chief."

Appalled at the error, Karen's eyes opened wide. She had to be careful, especially with the knowledge she had of their future. Luckily, Jumping Bull laughed and told her not to worry about her mistake. He padded the seat next to him and told her to sit. The feast was about to begin.

There was dancing, music, and laughter throughout the village with an abundance of every kind of food one could desire was placed before her. Those who could speak some English came to Karen. They spoke to her of their pleasure that she had saved their great chief. Some of the Indian women, who couldn't speak English, grabbed her and taught her how to do some of the dances. The feast went on until nightfall when the children were rushed to bed and it was just the men left to themselves.

Standing Deer approached Karen as she was leaving to go to sleep in Jumping Bull's lodge, asking her if she would return in the morning. He had been on her mind most of the night. She had managed to avoid him...until now. He informed her that at first sunlight they would be preparing for the Sun Dance ceremonies. Karen told him she hoped to return and backed away slowly.

Taking her hand, "Let us walk. It is a good night for a walk and I have not been able to spend time with you. It seems everyone wanted to be with the beautiful Karen."

Standing Deer and Karen walked quietly, hand in hand, through the woods toward the water. The singing of the night creatures and the pleasant coolness of the night surrounded them. Looking up to the heavens, she watched the stars twinkling high above. Feeling one with the earth, Mother Earth as the Indians called it, she understood how they felt about this land, the peacefulness and serenity that surrounded a person when they were here. It was wonderful.

She was fully aware that Standing Deer still held her hand. Karen felt like a thirteen year old experiencing her first love. Her hand felt small inside of his, the warmth of his skin went through her like an electrical pulse, and she could feel the surges going through her being. She kept reminding herself that she shouldn't be with him. Yet, she couldn't tear herself away.

Standing Deer stopped near the edge of the water. He had slowly and sensuously moved his hand up to touch her face lightly. He was awed by the halo of moonlight surrounding her hair, making it shimmer and shine like the many stars above him. Looking into Karen's eyes, he watched the gold inside of the brown twinkle like the gold rocks white men fought over. Ever so slowly and cautiously, he bent his head down to touch her lips.

Karen had taken a deep breath, her mind telling her no. She didn't move. She didn't want to move. With the first contact of their lips, she closed her eyes, and allowed herself to succumb to his touch, to this one moment. It was pure electricity. She felt the heated pulsation sweep through her body and soul. As he pressed harder, she melted into him.

Her conscience yelling she was wrong, was drowned out by the roar penetrating through her, like a freight train out of control. They were alone in the world. All she could feel was the burning heat from his lips and the coolness of his body against hers. It was like fire and water. As Standing Deer pulled away slowly, she could still feel the tingling sensation on her lips.

The betrayal of her body surprised her. Never had she felt her body shake from a passionate kiss or any other kind of sexual encounter. She had never been kissed like that before. No one had ever left her feeling so aware of a gentle, sensuous kiss, a kiss that invaded all of her being. No one ever left her so satisfied, yet, craving a desperate heated desire for more. She breathed a sigh of ecstasy and realized she had been holding her breath the whole time.

They stood there, still, in the passionate embrace that had left both of them breathless. Soon, the sounds of the world crept around them, slowly invaded their ears.

Karen was the first to break the embrace, feeling an immediate loss from the separation. Her eyes started to swell with water from unbidden, uncontrollable tears. Sadness engulfed her, haunting reality stopped her from going back into the comfort of his arms. She questioned herself for the first time in her life. How can something so beautiful be so undeniably wrong?

Looking up at Standing Deer, she could see confusion on his handsome face. She shook her head in a sad attempt to erase the swirling of her emotions, to stop the resistant tingling of her lips.

"This is wrong." She whispered, choked with heartfelt grief. Disgusted with herself, Karen turned and walked slowly away from Standing Deer. To her, it was the hardest thing she had ever had to do in her life.

Standing Deer was stunned. Didn't she feel the same? What was wrong? Did he do something wrong? A sense of loss engulfed him. Fear of her loss surrounded him like a pack of wolves.

"Did I dishonor you?" He called to her retreating back.

Karen stopped in mid-stride. Very aware of the betrayal of her body, she turned slowly around to face Standing Deer. She shook her head no, tears filled her eyes.

She could barely speak, her voice croaked. “I dishonored myself.”

Bewildered, Standing Deer watched as she walked away. His eyes didn’t leave her retreating back until she was no longer in his sight.

Chapter Six

Karen's despondency continued through her day and into the night. When she returned to Jumping Bull's lodge, she couldn't shake the feeling of sadness over the loss of Standing Deer. She kept asking herself repeatedly, why did he have to be married?

Alone in Jumping Bull's lodge, glad for the silence, she needed more time for herself. Bonnie understood her feelings of confusion. Indians sometimes took more than one wife, it was acceptable to them and their religious beliefs. Her explanations didn't help, it didn't change how she felt. A man having more than one wife wasn't acceptable.

Outside the lodge, she could hear excitement and movement. She recalled Standing Deer saying the preparation of the Sun Dance ceremonies was going to start today. Stretching, she prepared herself to go out into the new world.

Stepping into the sunlight, she observed the changes made to the village. Karen saw Two Feather's wife wave her arms to get her attention.

"Karreen! *Iho! Yau! Den u ye!*" Come here. Two Feather's wife waved her arms dramatically to help Karen understand. She smiled at the attempt to pronounce her name.

As she walked over to the lodge, she was amazed at the quick changes throughout the village. The men were erecting an extremely large lodge. She observed what appeared to be rafters inside, with poles leaning against them. There was a type of altar on the opposite side of what she appeared to be an entrance. Next to the side of the lodge poles, she could see the covering for the lodge. All the men worked as a team, each knowing exactly what he was supposed to do.

She was watching the men meticulously doing their work and bumped into an elderly woman. The woman snapped at her in Lakota and spit at her feet. Taken aback by the offensiveness of the gesture, Karen looked at the woman and said, "*Wanunhecun.*" Mistake. The elderly woman grunted at her and walked away.

Laughing Flower was aware of the confrontation and was impressed by the way Karen handled it. The old woman was a troublemaker.

When Karen arrived at the lodge, Laughing Flower pointed to herself and then to a flower. "*Wah,*" flower then she started laughing and said, "*Iha,*" laughing. She repeated the name together. "*Wah Iha.*"

It was the perfect name for the woman. She made an attempt to repeat her name. Patiently, she repeated her name a couple more times until Karen was able to say it properly. She would be able to pick up annunciating some of the words, sounds similar to the French language.

Laughing Flower proceeded to converse with sign language. Working together the rest of the day, she patiently helped Karen learn the ways of the people. The white woman was a joy to be with, she worked hard and learned fast.

During the afternoon, Laughing Flower noticed Karen watching Standing Deer, her eyes following him as he worked with the other warriors. When she scowled, Laughing Flower had touched her arm and raised her eyebrows in question. She couldn't understand how Standing Deer or his sisters could have possibly offended her new friend.

Knowing how Standing Deer felt about Karen, she knew he wouldn't intentionally hurt or offend her. She hadn't met his sisters yet, so it couldn't be them.

"What did Standing Deer do?"

Laughing Flower took Karen's arm and started to walk her over to Standing Deer's lodge where the three of them stood talking. Pulling her arm away, she said no. Perplexed, she pointed to Standing Deer and his sisters. Standing Deer could speak the white man's tongue and he should surely be able to clear up any misunderstandings.

Making another attempt to bring Karen over to Standing Deer's lodge, she pushed. "*Iho.*" Come. She pointed at the sisters and raised two fingers, "*Tanksitku, sha?*"

Karen raised her hands in frustration and confusion. Emphatically, she shook her head no. Karen knew sha meant yes, but what did tanksitku mean? Laughing Flower relented, but she knew the woman would try again.

Tense from frustration, it had not been easy avoiding Standing Deer when his lodge was only three lodges from Jumping Bull's. Whenever she saw him approaching, she would hurry away in the opposite direction. She knew she couldn't continue to avoid him. She would have to tell him she wasn't interested in a man who was already married. Then, if he had any respect for her feelings, he would leave her alone.

The next day Karen awoke with enthusiasm. Today was going to be a good day. She would be able to experience the Sun Dance first hand. She was curious to see if the information she received from the Internet was accurate.

It was also the day Bonnie was going to hang the canopy on the bed. They were both curious to see if it would stop her from returning home. Hopefully, when Bonnie took the canopy down she would return home and not be stuck in this other world. Karen was taking a big chance experimenting with the unknown.

A high pitched, terrifying scream pierced the tranquility within the lodge. Running out of the lodge, she found herself encircled by mass confusion. Across the village, near the water, Karen could see a woman holding a small child in her arms. Several people had surrounded the hysterical woman.

Running over to see what had happened, one look at the small child told the story. The child had gotten into the water and went under, her lungs filled with water. For how long?

She felt for a pulse, a very slight pulse that told her there was still time. Reaching to take the child out of the mother's arms, the woman started screaming hysterically again. The mother tried to hit Karen with her free hand.

Heart wrenching hysteria of the mother's screams jolted her into action. "Put the baby down"

Sitting Bull had been standing behind her and spoke to the woman. Humbly and carefully, the mother placed the little girl on the ground. She applied standard CPR techniques on the child.

Hushed murmurs circled the area until everyone watched in silence. Frantically, Karen worked harder and faster. Fear for the life of the small child kept her going. She was having a hard time reviving the child.

After a few moments, Sitting Bull knelt next to her and clumsily mimicked the motions, pumping the tiny girl's chest the way Karen had been doing. Together they continued until with much relief, the child spewed the water that had filled her lungs. Lifting the child over her knee face down, she used gravity to empty any excess water. The child started crying and the mother bent down and cradled her little girl in her arms.

She leaned her head against Sitting Bull, listening to the tears of relief from members of the tribe. They remained on the ground together, watching silently, relieved that she...they had succeeded.

The mother cradled the in her arms as she walked away. He spoke quietly. "You have done well. I would appreciate it if you would teach me how to do that."

"Of course I will, if you wish, and anyone else who would like to learn."

Sitting Bull smiled at Karen, needing to speak with her and knowing it wasn't the time. Excusing himself, she watched him approach Standing Deer. She made her way over to Laughing Flower. They had a considerable amount of preparations to make before the ceremonies. She could hear hushed whispers as she crossed the campsite, clueless to the disagreements circling the members of the tribe.

Standing Deer and Sitting Bull were discussing the council meeting the men had earlier. Some of the warriors were against Karen watching the Sun Dance. A white man or woman should never be able to watch. Jumping Bull was adamant that she was able to observe such a sacred ceremony. Everyone didn't agree until Jumping Bull told the council members that he believed she was sent by the Great Spirit. Jumping Bull explained to the council that she had denied being the daughter of the Great Spirit. He believed she was sent by Him, telling the warriors of the powers and great medicine she possessed.

This morning Karen had proved it to everyone.

Standing Deer asked if he could join Sitting Bull when he spoke to Karen about the ceremony. After he explained his blunder with Karen, Sitting Bull understood why he was concerned, but couldn't understand why Standing Deer would believe he wasn't a good enough warrior to marry the daughter of the Great Spirit.

Walking over to Two Feather's lodge, Sitting Bull reviewed everything Standing Deer had told him and what was discussed about Karen in the council meeting. Hearing him call, she turned and saw the two warriors approach the lodge.

Silently, Karen listened to Sitting Bull explain to her about the council and their decision. She was surprised to learn the white man wasn't allowed to watch the Sun Dance, and equally surprised at their decision to allow her to attend. After he finished explaining about the importance of the Sun Dance, he looked at Standing Deer and then at her and told them they needed to talk, leaving them alone. Karen tried to stop him but he shook his head and walked to Jumping Bull's lodge. Standing Deer had somehow finagled Sitting Bull into talking to her.

With a clenched heart, she looked at Laughing Flower for assistance. Sitting inside the lodge, Laughing Flower shook her head and continued tending to the baby. She did not like being manipulated and the fierce warrior standing before her would not deter how she felt. If he was going to push, she would have to give him a piece of her mind.

Determined, she placed both hands on her hips. "Listen to me real good Standing Deer, because I'm not going to repeat myself." A stern note to her voice, "I will not lower myself and dishonor myself by getting involved with a married man. I don't care what the Indians believe. I will not be subjected to such atrocities! I cannot, in anyway, understand how you could actually believe I would tolerate such disgusting behavior. The other night was a huge, inexplicable, mistake! I'm disgusted with my own behavior. It was totally unacceptable. I allowed my emotions to control my behavior. I will not allow it to happen again."

Crossing her arms, she looked directly into Standing Deer's eyes, and took a deep breath. "I will not be in this village long. I want you to stay away from me. Don't talk to me. Don't come near me. Just leave me alone!" She turned to walk toward Laughing Flower when he grabbed her arm, his face red with anger.

"Now, wait a minute." Speaking through clenched teeth, a vein pulsed on his forehead. "I listened to you, now you listen to me," squeezing her arm harder. "I have no wives. I don't have a woman or women. Not all Indians have more than one wife. Where did you get the idea that I was married?"

She grabbed his wrist, trying to break free. Standing Deer looked at her in irritation, waiting for a response.

"Let me go!"

Eyeing Laughing Flower openmouthed behind Standing Deer, she saw the shock written on her face at her behavior to openly dishonor and humiliate Standing Deer by speaking to him in such a way in front of the whole village. Karen was too angry to care.

"I didn't mean to dishonor you the other night. If you had given me the chance, I would have done something to show you I was sorry." Leaning closer, he growled, "Don't ever speak to me in that manner, in front of my people or anyone, again. I will leave you alone, if that is what you wish." He let go of her arm and crossed his arms. When she didn't respond he walked away, satisfied with the look of mortification on her face.

Putting her hand over her mouth as she stood, watching him walk away, she was crestfallen, humiliated, and certainly forced to eat a serious helping of humble pie. Many years ago her father had told her that most disagreements happen because of a misunderstanding.

Not married? Who were those women? If that was true, then they had a chance. Oh, no. No, no, no. She had ruined everything!

It wouldn't work. They were literally from two very distinct, separate worlds. How could it possibly work out for the two of them?

She turned and walked over to Jumping Bull's lodge, the flaps were down, and she pursed her lips. As she was staring at the entrance, unsure of what to do next, Sitting Bull came up behind her.

"Did you need something, Karen?"

"I'm sorry to bother you," rubbing her wrist, "But can you tell me what tank...tanksi...tanksitku means?"

"Sister," immediately enlightened by the cause of Karen's behavior toward Standing Deer, "his younger sisters."

Feeling foolish, Karen thanked Sitting Bull. She knew better, making assumptions, allowing them to develop into a very gross injustice toward Standing Deer. She still believed they couldn't pursue a relationship, but knew she owed him an apology. The ceremony would be beginning soon and everyone was absorbed in his or her final preparations. Her search for Standing Deer would have to wait.

Sitting Bull and Jumping Bull had spoken to each other about the attraction they saw between Standing Deer and Karen, concluding that the two of them were meant for each other. Jumping Bull had told Sitting Bull it would be quite entertaining, watching the two of them.

Jumping Bull was curious why Karen asked what sister meant. Sitting Bull shook his head, she thought Standing Deer was married, didn't know the women his sisters. White women were very possessive when it came to their man. They didn't want to share with anyone, especially another woman. Somehow, she must have gotten the impression that Standing Deer was married.

Jumping Bull grinned, a good healthy bout of jealousy could be a good thing, telling his son he believed Standing Deer would have his hands full with that little one. The father and son finished their final preparations, exiting the lodge to commence the sacred ceremony.

Standing, out of the way, near Jumping Bull's lodge she watched, curious to see if the research she had read was accurate, her eyes darting around the camp. The sacred drums thundered, the rhythm mimicked the heartbeat in her chest.

The drums suddenly stopped. Sitting Bull entered the center of the village and conducted the prayers and blessings.

The dancing and music began again with several men from other tribes joining in the ceremony. Laughing Flower along with Standing Deer's sisters joined Karen. The women took several moments to explain how to pronounce their names and what they meant. Sunshine in the Morning was adept at sign language, introducing Yellow Bird as their friend.

As usual, she had many questions. Karen pointed to a man sitting next to Jumping Bull.

"He is Many Horses. He is from the Oglala Sioux. Many Horses is here to watch Crazy Horse attend the Sun Dance." Sunshine in the Morning turned and pointed. "The young warrior right there dancing in the circle is Crazy Horse."

"There are many men here and families. Is it common to have warriors from other tribes join in the ceremony?" At this time Standing Deer had joined the women. Karen jumped at the opportunity and had made her apologies to him. The women discreetly left the two alone, letting him answer her questions.

"Yes, we are all Sioux, Lakota, Nakota, and Dakota tribes, as well as the Cheyenne. Although we don't live in the same village, we join for the Sun Dance ceremonies. Over there is Sleeping Elk, and next to him is his brother Black Bear."

Explaining the ritual steps of the Sun Dance, how it would last hours, the young men fasting before the performance of the ceremony, he pointed to the young warriors who were dancing and staring at the sun until they received their visions. The young man's warrior society would dance, if they chose, to assist their friends in obtaining his vision.

He pointed out the forks that would be used for the participants, thrust through the breast muscles of the dancers. They would strain against it until they tore loose.

She reached up and outlined the scars on his chest with her fingers.

Nodding his head, "Yes, I have participated in the Sun Dance." He continued explaining the ceremony. "Before they enter the ceremonial lodge, they must dance around and pretend to go inside four times. It's essential for them to do this in order for them to receive the blessed visions they seek.

Karen wanted but couldn't look away. She stood mesmerized as she watched the young warriors. Appalled, disgusted, fascinated, she couldn't fathom why anyone would want to put themselves through such physical and mental torture. Couldn't they find another way? Something a bit more civilized?

Several hours had passed, one by one, the young warriors came out of the ceremonial lodge and collapsed into the arms of their friends. A murmur floated throughout the village. There was one young warrior left.

Standing Deer had been over with Two Feather's when Karen waved him over to her.

"He is younger than the others. Will they stop it?" she asked him.

"No. It would be Red Cloud's decision to stop it and he wouldn't dishonor him. Crazy Horse is a strong warrior. He will do it." Standing Deer whispered. "And, he isn't that young."

More warriors entered the circle to dance. They wanted to encourage the brave warrior. All Karen could hear was the beat of the drums and the hushed murmur of the people.

Finally, Crazy Horse broke through, collapsing into Red Cloud's arms. Standing nearby, Many Horses nodded his approval.

Instead of guiding him to his lodge, Red Cloud yelled out. "Where is the white woman from the mountains?"

Karen stood frozen, ears buzzing, stunned by the outburst. The village was silent, some searched the area for the woman. Standing Deer guided her to Red Cloud. He was holding onto Crazy Horse, helping him stand on his feet.

Crazy Horse looked at her, speaking quietly as he gasped for breath. His eyes were filled with pain and anger. His voice was hoarse as he spoke slowly, with an importance of a message he believed was from the Great Spirit.

What was so important that he had to tell her immediately? Couldn't it have waited?

Since Crazy Horse had refused to learn and speak the white man's tongue, Standing Deer interpreted for them.

"These words are from the vision the Great Spirit has given me. You have come from a world beyond. Your powers are great. Use them wisely. Be careful of what you know. Life must continue, as it should be. Don't try to change anything. This I say to you. Learn the ways of the Indian and be there when you are needed."

He paused and closed his eyes, "Listen to me Spirit of the Mountain. Crazy Horse would never want to have to walk in your moccasins and know the things that you know."

Crazy Horse passed out and Red Cloud took him away to administer the wounds the young man had received in the ceremony. The village was quiet until Jumping Bull yelled to continue the great celebration.

Karen's heart raced. How could he know such things? Was there something to this ceremony? What did Crazy Horse see in his vision? What does he know?

Chapter Seven

Telling Standing Deer that she wanted to be alone, Karen decided to take a stroll along the same path he had shown her the night they kissed.

So many confusing questions were going through her analytical mind. There were too many questions and not enough answers, just theories, theories of supernatural powers. With everything that has happened to her, she had proof that supernatural powers have been around a long time.

How did Crazy Horse know what he did? Was there something to this ritual the Indians performed? What did he know? How was she going to deal with this? Everything he had said to her made her believe how powerful these rituals could actually be.

She was astonished at the knowledge he had learned in the Sun Dance ceremony. How did he know she was from a different world? How did he get the information? Crazy Horse's genuine warning made her wary.

Be careful of what you know. Life must continue, as it should be. Words and warnings Crazy Horse believed were from the Great Spirit. Don't try to change anything. Would she? Could she? What would it do to the future or past if she did? Was the past considered the present if she is living in it? Sighing, shook her head in confusion.

She wasn't sure what year it was, but knew thousands and thousands of Americans and hopeful immigrants would be coming to the western plains. The destruction of the great Indian Nation would be imminent, out of her control.

What could she possibly do to change history? Probably, quite a bit. She could warn them of impending wars. They would be better prepared, saving unnecessary loss of lives. Thousands of innocent people could be spared. Would it just prolong the inevitable? By warning them, would it make it worse and completely destroy the Indian Nation? She was better off leaving things as they were, as they are. At least, this way she knew where her worlds belonged.

Now, she understood why he wouldn't want to "walk in her moccasins." A cliché she heard for years but never really expected to happen to her.

Karen became so absorbed in her thoughts that she didn't realize she had left the protection and confines of the village far behind. She continued walking, deep in thought, blind to everything about her. Karen was hearing the message from Crazy Horse repeating itself, over and over in her mind.

She didn't see the camp of the white traders hidden behind the brush. Seeing her, a white woman unescorted so close to an Indian camp, they decided that was a captive. Obviously, she was a very trusted whore or they wouldn't have let her wonder around outside of the village. A captive who was allowed that type of freedom was taking good care of their savage needs.

Karen heard muted laughter but didn't think anything of it.

One of the men pointed and whispered, "Let's have some fun. They wouldn't care if we took her and used her for a while. She opened her legs wide and willingly for the savages, and will do the same for us."

The trapper slowly and quietly followed her. He waited for his chance, hit her over the head with a rock, and dragged her back to the camp like a sack of potatoes.

After a few moments, Karen became conscious. She was groggy and lightheaded with a searing pain in the back of her head. She felt a burning liquid being shoved down her throat. Groggily, she thought it tasted like whiskey. It was foul, burning her throat as it went down. Gagging, she tried pulling away but someone pulled on her hair and forced her mouth open. She had no choice but to swallow. The harsh liquid burned her throat, leaving her in a drunken daze. She was laid back onto the hard ground. The ground was moving, spinning.

Karen began feeling hands all over her body. They were touching her everywhere, so many hands.

Two mouths suckled her breasts. She tried pushing them away but couldn't control her movements. Her arms felt so heavy. She had no control of her movements, no strength. She was drunk. One of them spoke to her and asked her if she was ready for some fun. Bleary eyed, she turned to where the voice had come. Helpless, she felt one of them fumbling on top of her before she blessedly passed out from the shock of absorbing so much liquor in her system in such a short time.

Karen felt nauseous, aching everywhere, her head felt as if it was exploding. Every available place on her body had been manhandled, bile crept into her throat and knew she was going to get sick. Leaning over, she emptied the contents of what was left in her stomach.

Anger seized her and seemed to take a permanent hold. How dare they do this to her! Hatred and anger swallowed her. Total, unadulterated anger enveloped her. She wanted to destroy these men. But first, Karen decided she would torture them. She would start with the one who had asked her if she wanted to have some fun. She would show him some fun!

Anger controlled her emotions and actions. Her kinetic abilities took control. She didn't consider that she was a doctor and was supposed to save lives. She wanted to punish them and punish them she would. She wanted them all dead.

She heard a muted gurgling sound, rolling over she held herself up on shaky arms. Karen pictured herself choking the man who had spoken to her. In her mind, she pushed him against a tree and repeatedly banged his head against the trunk of the tree. She slowly, dizzily, turned her head, watching him trying to stop the invisible hands from choking him. In a panic, he tried to run away, yelling something about her being a witch. She laughed an unforgiving sick laugh. She didn't care. She wanted revenge. She wanted him in pain. She wanted all of them in unmistakable, torturous pain. She smiled as she sensed that their little camp was in a frenzy.

A familiar voice distracted her. She stopped torturing the trader and watched with complete satisfaction as he killed the man, controlled by hatred she felt elated with Standing Deer's rescue.

Looking around, she saw that he had killed the men, four men, who had defiled her and deserved to die.

He yanked his knife out of the chest of one of the last traders, stabbing the knife into the dirt and methodically cleaned the knife on the grass. In shock Karen felt as if she was watching him from a distance, in a dream. She started getting cold and everything around her seemed to slow itself in waves.

Walking over to her slowly, he took her and held her in his arms, waiting for the tears to come. He whispered softly to her and kissed her face, holding her as he would a hurt child.

She was beginning to feel numb. "I...I want...to...to take...a bath." she barely whispered.

He carried her over to the water and tried to help her undress. Karen pulled away with such a ferocity of anger that he helplessly stepped away as he watched her struggle to take the torn dress off. Slowly, she immersed herself in the water, feeling the cool clear water gradually covering her body. Her body, that had been defiled, needed the coolness of the water. All she wanted to do was wash the disgrace and filth away. She kept submerging her head under the water. She repeatedly grabbed the gritty dirt and sand from the bottom and scrubbed her body with it.

Standing Deer watched silently. Frustrated, his heart was breaking for her. He had followed her to make sure she was safe. When he realized that she had passed the village perimeters, he was going to make himself known to her.

Stupid white men, should have known she wouldn't have been walking outside the village alone and unescorted. It was lucky that he had gotten there in time. Blinding fury had taken control when he saw them pour the whiskey down her throat. The closest trapper was dead before they even realized he was in their camp. The trapper who had tried to mount her was next.

Didn't they know that all people should be treated with respect? It was becoming a vicious circle. White men raped and killed the Indian women, so the Indian raped and killed the white woman. Who cares who started it? When was it all going to stop?

He watched as she submerged herself repeatedly and came up with fistfuls of dirt and sand to cleanse her skin. Her motions of cleansing had started slow but as time continued her actions became quicker and more frantic. Her cleansing became harder and faster, the frustration of the ordeal came out in Karen's actions. Her skin was becoming raw from the scrubbing.

He had to stop her. Entering the water, he lifted her up. She resisted him with a viciousness, uncharacteristic of her personality. With both fists she pummeled him until he fell back into the water. Sputtering he grabbed her from underneath and started carrying her to the shore.

She pounded his back in fury. "No, I have to get it off! I need to wash it all away. They were filthy. Lord only knows the last time they had a bath. Those men were probably diseased. I know damn well they didn't use protection." She ferociously rubbed herself.

Putting her down on the shore, he held her hands to her sides. With a strained, tremulous voice, she explained to Standing Deer, "I've never had unprotected sex. What if they had STD's? What if they got me pregnant? I believe abortions should be legal, but I can't have one. I don't believe that it is right for me."

Karen felt angry, frustrated, and dirty. There were no tears yet. She still didn't feel remorse for the dead men. Perhaps she never would.

She was bleeding from the sand and had silt embedded in the cuts. Grabbing her hands with one of his, he rinsed the sand from her wounds with his free hand. She still hadn't looked at him.

"I need penicillin. Oh God! Bonnie's putting up the canopy tonight. I can't stay now. I need to go home. I have to get medicine." Finally, the tears came.

Karen pounded the ground racked with tears. She screamed hysterically, "I want to forget!"

As she cried, Standing Deer took her into his arms and rocked her. He stroked her hair, speaking to her in soft tones to calm her. She wasn't making any sense to him. STD? Bonnie...canopy...pennies? What in the world could she be talking about? Why would she need the white man's money?

He walked her over to the edge of the water and put the dress on her. He was angry with himself and saddened as he watched her. She stood there looking defeated, like a beaten helpless child.

They started walking along the banks of the water. The silence was deafening. Standing Deer was worried for her mind. She just walked with her head down, blind to everything around her. After a time, without saying a word to Standing Deer, Karen stopped and sat down. Standing Deer sat next to her.

"I'm not ready to go back to the village."

Standing Deer nodded his head and remained silent. He put his arm carefully around her and held her gently against the side of his chest. She closed her eyes feeling protected in his arms. She mumbled to him that she was tired. He laid back, pulling her with him and she laid her head on his shoulders.

Chapter Eight

Bonnie let herself into the house with the key Karen had given her. Putting the mail on the kitchen table, she watered the plants her friend had scattered around the house. As she went from room to room, she pictured the wonderful time Karen was having. She returned the pitcher to the sink drain and entered the bedroom to hang the canopy. The box would be on the chaise lounge.

Opening the door, she was startled to see two people sleeping. What was he doing here and why was she back?

Touching her softly so she wouldn't startle her, she waited for Karen to open her eyes. Bonnie excitedly pointed to the other side of the bed. Puzzled, Karen turned around with wide eyes. Standing Deer was lying next to her asleep in the bed.

Whispering to Bonnie as she crept out of the bed, "Holy cow, now what am I going to do?"

"Oh! He is a hunk. Oh goodness, you did him no justice at all when you described him to me."

Karen and Bonnie silently tiptoed out of the room, leaving Standing Deer asleep on the bed. He would awaken soon but she needed to talk to Bonnie as soon as possible.

"He is gorgeous! You're right, he is built like Apollo. Are you sure you wouldn't want to be one of his wives?"

"Standing Deer isn't married." she replied, an unusual dullness in her voice.

Squinting her eyes Bonnie asked, "What's wrong?"

"Let me have some coffee first. I also need you to go to the pharmacy for me. I can't leave him here and I can't take him with me." Karen sighed. She was glad Bonnie was a counselor and a good friend. She really needed someone to talk to.

Quickly telling the story from beginning to end, Bonnie waited silently until she was finished. Just as she was going to speak, they heard Standing Deer calling. Karen filled out a prescription for herself, gave Bonnie some money, and sent her on her way. Standing Deer wasn't ready for Bonnie yet, not for all that energy coming at him all at once. Laughing Flower and Bonnie were very much alike.

Standing Deer was sitting up, eyes wide in astonishment. He was staring at the digital clock, watching the timer blinking. At least she had some idea of what to expect in his world but he had no concept of hers.

"Is this your world?" Curiously looking about the room, "Where am I?"

"You are here." grinning at the memory of their first encounter. He returned her grin, laughing at her witticism.

This was going to be an adventure. Walking over to the closet, she pulled out a pair of shorts her ex, David, had left behind. She handed them to Standing Deer. Opening the bureau drawer, she pulled out a T-shirt. Twirling the shorts around in his hand, and looking at them with a puzzled look, she explained to him to take his loincloth off and put the shorts on with the pockets to the front. She shut the door and left him to change.

When Standing Deer was finished, he walked over to the door and tried to open it. He traced his fingers along the crack before he pulled on the doorknob but nothing happened. He tried a few more times until he finally called for Karen.

Karen opened the door, showing him how to turn the knob in order for the door to open. The shorts fit him well. They just looked odd with his knife strategically placed at the waist.

"You have a strange world."

"Oh, you haven't seen anything yet."

Following Karen through the house to the kitchen, his eyes darted around, absorbing everything around him. He stopped and felt the roughness of the textured walls. They didn't bend or move when touched. Her lodge had strange walls with paintings surrounded by wood for decoration. Why didn't she just paint the pictures on the walls?

He felt the carpet underneath his feet and looked down. What kind of animal had it come from? Wiggling his toes, the fur didn't feel very soft on the feet. Cloth on the walls throughout the lodge, stopped the light of the sun from coming in. When they arrived in the kitchen, he felt a cool breeze coming from the ceiling. Looking up and saw a shiny, square object with holes in it. Raising his hand, he felt the cool air blowing against his palm.

"You must be very important in your world to have such a big lodge. Where is the rest of your family?"

Karen didn't respond right away. Instead, she handed him a cup of coffee and asked if he wanted to go outside on the patio. As they went outside to the patio, she was relieved she decided to put up a privacy fence.

"My family lives out of state.

"What is out of state?" he asked curiously. There was a lot he could ask. He wasn't sure what he could or couldn't ask without offending her.

"It's like a territory, only it all belongs to one country."

Standing Deer partially understood but as they reached the patio and he saw the pool, all other questions fled his mind. He walked over to the pool and submerged his hand in the water. He felt the coolness and wondered why she would keep her drinking water in such a strange and large enclosure. Didn't she live near a lake or stream? Where were the fish?

Standing Deer stood up and looked around the yard. It appeared as if someone had taken plants and placed them in an order. Nothing grew freely here. He didn't recognize any of the plants. It seemed to be a pleasant piece of land except for the fact that they didn't let the plants grow where the hand of the Great Spirit placed them. Here on this piece of land he couldn't see any plants she could use.

This piece of land surrounded her lodge like the white man's fort. It hid her land from the other strange lodges that he could see beyond her fort. Why would she want to be closed off from her own people? Did the white man in her world fear each other so much that they had to secure themselves behind wooden walls? Was her world that dangerous that she had to hide behind a barricade? No wonder the white man doesn't trust the Indian. How could they if they have to live like this? They can't trust their own people. How could they learn to trust something that was different to them?

Standing Deer jumped at the loud, unfamiliar screeching sound he heard from the sky. "Run!" His knife was in hand as he was dragging her to the door. Why wasn't she reacting to this danger?

Karen was more focused on the dance of emotions and questions she saw flitter on his face. She wasn't paying attention to the jet overhead. She grabbed his arm and attempted to stop him from running into the house, understanding that it was pure instinct for him to react in the manner he did.

"It's an airplane. It is used for transportation." Karen felt dismayed. She had a lot of explaining to do in the next several hours. She took a deep breath, looking toward the sky wondering how she got into this mess.

She needed to explain some of this modern world to Standing Deer. He would at least be partially knowledgeable about this world, although he wouldn't be here long. How much she should explain she wasn't certain.

Deciding to start with something within his sight, "This is a pool. It helps a person keep cool, refreshed, and I swim in it." Tapping her lip, "You don't drink it."

He shook his head. He understood what she had said but couldn't understand the necessity of needing one next to your lodge.

"This is for you only?" Scanning her lodge surrounded by fort walls.

"Yes."

"You use it only for bathing?"

"No, just for swimming. I have bathtubs for bathing." Biting her lip, she realized that she wasn't explaining properly. "Maybe you should just ask me as many questions as you want. If I can, I will answer you."

Standing Deer was relieved to have her permission to pursue his questions. To the Lakota, it was rude to ask personal questions without the consent of the other person. So many questions, he wasn't sure where to start. Finally, he decided to start with the Karen's lodge and land. For about an hour, Karen diligently answered his questions. Bonnie returned just as he asked her if he could see more of the city.

Calling to Karen as she walked through the house, Bonnie looked in the den first, and then went straight to the back patio.

"Hello." Bonnie said in a singsong voice. Looking at Standing Deer, "it is a pleasure to meet you. I have heard a lot about you. I'm Bonnie." She looked at Karen "Your package is on the kitchen table."

"Thank you."

"So tell me, Standing Deer, what do you think of our world? Do you like it so far? Would you like to see more? Maybe you would like to stay for a few days? Or..."

"Bonnie, stop! He's only been here an hour. I don't think it would be wise if he saw anything else. And, it certainly wouldn't be a good idea if he stayed for a few days!" Karen was irritated at Bonnie's typical burst of energy.

"Why not?" Bonnie was bubbling with her usual energy. "It would be great. Just imagine what it would be like for him to see all of this..."

"And imagine," Karen cut her off. "Just imagine how he will have to deal with the all this knowledge, the different technology. Wouldn't that be amazing?" Karen shook her head. Sometimes she wondered where Bonnie left her common sense.

Bonnie blinked, bewildered by the rudeness coming out of her friend's mouth.

"I don't think it would be wise if he saw anything else. And it certainly wouldn't be a good idea if he stayed for a few days."

"We could take him to all the sights. We are in Orlando. People travel from all over the world to come here. We could take him to the Seminole reservation."

"No! What are you thinking? We can't take him to the reservation. That's unfair! He shouldn't see too much. He's not a guest from out of state, you know. How do you think he would react if he saw a reservation?" Karen shook her head angrily at Bonnie. What could she possibly be thinking?

"Excuse me," said Standing Deer. "You seem to be speaking as if I'm not here. Do I not have a say in what is to be decided?"

"No." Karen replied.

"Yes, you do." Bonnie said. "Karen, don't you think you should get out of those clothes and put something on that is more up to date? Aren't you hot?"

Karen looked down at the torn deer skin dress and realized she wasn't hot. She had been so comfortable that she forgot she was still in the Indian mode of dress.

"I'll go change. I need to grab a bite to eat and take that medication anyway. Anyone else hungry?" Karen asked, "sandwiches?" She went inside to change and make lunch to bring out to the patio.

As Karen was changing, she realized that Bonnie had manipulated the situation by changing the subject to her dress. She moved as quickly as humanly possible wondering why and what Bonnie was up to.

Standing Deer was alert and aware that the woman before him managed to get the two of them alone. A striking woman, her hair was a golden brown, cut short like a white man's, her light brown eyes flickered in the sun, exaggerating the high energy and sincerity in the woman.

"Are you a medicine woman like Karen?"

"No, not really. We are both healers in our own way. I have a doctorate but it's in theology. I have my master's degree in psychology. I heal people's minds. She heals their bodies."

She was excited to be here with this man from the past. Uncomfortable with the ensuing silence, Bonnie asked a question she had been desperately wanting to ask. "Sooooo, Standing Deer, you aren't married."

"No." He didn't wish to explain why he didn't have a woman. It wasn't the way of the Lakota to speak of the dead. He understood she didn't have the knowledge of the Lakota way. "What is theology?"

"Theology is the study of religions, faith, and beliefs." When he didn't respond, Bonnie continued, "Not married. That's so great!" Tilting his head, she realized she needed to quantify. "I mean, it's great that you aren't married."

He raised his eyebrow, penetrating her with an indulgent stare.

"Karen's very interested in you. It really upset her when she thought you were married to those squaws."

Bonnie wanted to play matchmaker, until she saw his face fill with anger and tension. Puzzled by his reaction she wondered what she had said to offend him.

"Did I offend you?" She asked, confused by his quick change in demeanor.

"Those squaws as you have described them, are my sisters and their friend. It is an insult to call an Indian woman a squaw."

Bonnie was flabbergasted. "I'm so sorry! I had no idea. I won't make that mistake again."

Standing Deer nodded his head in acceptance of her apology believing that it was sincere. Smiling, he leaned forward, "Does she have a mate?"

"No. She doesn't have a mate. Marriage has always been a "someday" with her."

"You think she is interested in me? That makes my heart cheer. I have decided to marry her."

Bonnie laughed. "Oh, this is going to be a good adventure!" Obviously, he was determined to be her husband. "You will have a hard time convincing her that your marriage would work. She believes there will be a major conflict because you are from two separate worlds. I wish you luck because she'll fight this love she feels for you as much as she can."

Karen came out with a platter of sandwiches. She didn't miss the heads close together in conversation. She knew Bonnie well enough to know that she had something up her sleeve.

After they finished their sandwiches, Bonnie started talking about letting him see the city.

"I agree Standing Deer shouldn't see the reservation. You're right. It would be confusing and possibly traumatic. But, I see no reason why you can't take him for a ride in the car and let him see some of the sights. Also, if it isn't inconvenient for him, I don't see any harm in having him stay overnight, at least one night." Bonnie looked at Karen and added. "It would be a good way to test the canopy."

Karen sighed. Hesitantly she looked over to Standing Deer. "What do you think?"

"I would like to see your world. It will help me know you better. The ceremonies will continue without me, but I cannot stay away for too long. Many Horses told us he saw white soldiers and Pawnee while they were traveling to the village."

Out-voted, she relented. "Fine, but only one night."

Bonnie was exalted. She only had two appointments this afternoon and she would be able to join them. She had loads of questions for Standing Deer. Bonnie started babbling about all the different places they could go when her phone rang. Excusing herself, she went inside to make the call.

Standing Deer watched warily as she stood and talked to no one he could see. What was that thing in her hand? Why was she talking to it?

She never realized how wonderful modern luxuries were until you saw them through someone else's eyes. The telephone was such a common object. He was like a child discovering the world around him. She had to remind herself that this was a new world to him. Explaining the telephone and its uses, she told him it was a common tool for communication and that nearly all homes had one or more.

There was so much magic surrounding him and Karen's world took it so casually. Was her world so large that she needed so much magic to survive?

Bonnie told Karen she had a minor crisis to take care of and she would try to get back as soon as possible. The two of them discussed Bonnie returning to put the canopy up so Karen could stay with the Lakota. They agreed on the day and time.

Standing Deer detected a vigilance with their words. That appeared to be normal for Karen, but believed it was difficult for Bonnie. Bonnie had said something about the future and Karen had reprimanded her. She told Bonnie to be careful on how she worded things, emphasizing that she would be returning to the present world, not the future, nor the past. Apologizing, she looked over to Standing Deer to see if he noticed her slip of the tongue. He had, but Standing Deer was wise enough not to show it.

Their words made no sense. What future were they referring to? What did they mean by returning to the present world? Or was it the past that they had said? The more they spoke with hidden meanings, the more he felt confused.

Standing Deer was relieved when Bonnie left. He liked her well enough, but he wanted to be alone with Karen. If she was right about Karen having feelings for him, he needed time to convince her that their love would survive between the two worlds.

Now that he had seen her world, he felt somewhat unsure of himself. With all this magic around her, why would she want to leave her world to be with him? She was accustomed to all this magic, all the time. What could he give her besides himself? Would his way of life be good enough? Standing Deer had a terrible feeling there was a lot more magic than what he had seen so far. If she would be willing, how much would he be asking her to give up?

Karen thought it felt good, natural, to have Standing Deer here with her. The magnetism she had felt when she first met him was still very strong. Even as they sat there in their own private thoughts, she could still feel the electricity pulsing between the two of them.

Maybe, it could work. Would he want to give up his life on the prairie? He probably wouldn't have to. They could leave the canopy off the bed and she could put it away somewhere. They could live between the two worlds. Bea's parents did it. Their marriage survived, proving it was possible.

She shook her head dismayed at her own thoughts. Karen wanted to be with him for the rest of their lives. With so much conflict between the whites and the Indians in his world, it just wouldn't work. She felt like the rope in a fierce game of tug-of-war. What she greatly desired and what she felt was best were two very different things.

However, if fate had brought them together, she wouldn't be able to fight it anyway. She should see what happens, one day at a time.

Deciding to go for a swim, she stood and asked Standing Deer if he would like to take a swim in the pool as well. He agreed and she excused herself to change into her bathing suit.

When she returned, towels in hand, Standing Deer stood, taking off the shorts and shirt, comfortable in his bare skin. She took in a deep breath, her heart raced, and she feared he could see it pounding through her chest. Reveling in the eye candy before her, she enjoyed every inch of the massive, magnificent body before her.

Her body hummed with desire. She watched him take the feathers out of his hair and put them on the table. Turning around, he went into the water, his muscles flexing with each graceful movement.

What she didn't see was his grin and the look of satisfaction on his face. It pleased him greatly to know she was attracted to him.

He swam to the deep end and called to her. "Are you coming or are you going to stand there watching me?"

Laughing, Karen put the towels down and dove into the invigorating waters of the deep end. Standing Deer was playful and knew how to have fun. The world around them disappeared. They were the only two in existence.

She had forgotten that he was naked until they were in the shallow end of the pool. He had pulled her to him and kissed her. She could feel his nakedness against her belly. Her being was aflame with a fire burning with the desire she had felt before, a burning desire she had felt with him and only with him. She began to succumb to their overwhelming need for each other when she recalled the traders. She went stone cold and pulled away.

He felt her instant withdrawal. "What is wrong?"

"Those traders, we can't. Besides, I don't have any protection. We can't make love yet. It wouldn't be safe and I'm not ready. We're going too fast."

Standing Deer shook his head in dismay. "A woman should never have to experience such an ordeal. I'm sorry that you had to go through that. Your first time with a man shouldn't be pushed on you in that way. It is a good thing I had gotten there when I did. They were cruel and disgusting but did not have the chance to take you."

"What? What do you mean they didn't take me?"

"I followed you to make sure you were safe. The trapper was drunk on the white man's whiskey, fumbling like an idiot. I took care of him before he had the chance to take your virginity."

"He never penetrated me? Didn't enter me?"

"No."

Tears filled her eyes.

"Do not shed tears my love. It is over now." He spoke deeply, passionately and with true feelings. "Let me show you what it is like for a man and woman to share their love properly. I want to make love with you and show you the tenderness and power that love can give two people."

"I wasn't a virgin Standing Deer. I've had sex before." Sniffing with relief, "I wasn't raped. It came so close, too close. Those men have scarred me for life."

"Why did you stop me before if you weren't a virgin? I thought I had offended you. I thought I had dishonored you."

"Because I'm the type of person who takes things slow. Rushing into a relationship causes heartache. I rushed into a relationship before and I don't want to make the same mistake again. Please, you need to understand." Licking her lips, "With you, our worlds are so very far apart. We come from two separate and distant lives. I don't know how we would be able to have a relationship with each other. Even though I desire to love you, it scares me because of the conflicts that our people have had and will have. I'm sorry. I can't make love right now. I'm just not ready."

Standing Deer pulled her into his arms. "When you are ready and willing, we can make it work. You are a very strong woman. I cannot see you failing at anything."

"Well, I have. When I make mistakes, I make big mistakes. Besides, there are other reasons why we can't make love."

Standing Deer laughed. "So what are your other excuses?"

He didn't play emotional games. That's why she enjoyed his company so much. So far, Standing Deer was honest and down to earth, something she admired and respected in a person.

Feigning indignation, "They aren't excuses. They are legitimate reasons." In earnest, she continued. "I don't just jump into bed with anyone who comes along. I don't have a lot of experience like some women. It is unwise to have unprotected sex. Better to avoid diseases and pregnancy that way, don't you think? We need to use protection. And most of all I'm not ready. Don't push me."

"Forgive me. I should be more understanding to your feelings. What is this protection you are talking about?"

"It's called a condom." Karen explained. "You put it on your penis and it protects the man and woman from getting any possible diseases, and from getting pregnant."

"Well then," he laughed, "when you are ready. If that is what you desire, we will get an abundance of protection."

Standing Deer picked her up and threw her into the deep end of the pool. While they waited for Bonnie to return the two of them played in the pool satisfied to spend time with each other.

Chapter Nine

Bonnie called and said she was unable to return but she would put the canopy on the bed within a few days. They decided to go for a ride in the car and show him some of the sights.

She showed him where the bathroom was and how to use it. She grinned as he continued flushing the chain, the little shiny handle that made the water disappear entertained and fascinated him. Where did the water go? He tried lifting the bowl to see where it went but it appeared to be attached to the floor. He discovered the water inside the tank and focused several times on how it worked. Interesting, it was a strange and unusual device her people used to relieve themselves. One didn't have to leave the lodge to relieve themselves.

As they were entering the garage, Karen explained to him what a car was and why it was a necessary mode of transportation.

They hadn't left the housing division yet when Standing Deer started moving around and looking underneath the seats and in the glove box. Karen warily looked at him out of the corners of her eyes. "What are you doing?"

"Where are the people?"

"What people? What are you talking about?"

"I hear voices singing. Do you have little people hidden in the car somewhere?"

"Voices?" She took so much for granted. "The radio! Right here." She pointed toward the radio/cd player. "You turn it on and off like this. You can change channels and pick different stations to listen to if you don't like what they are playing. It's another form of communication." Karen smiled, "Except you can't talk back to it."

Standing Deer nodded his head and started fiddling with the buttons. He accidentally pushed the volume button to the highest setting. The car reverberated in sound. He jumped, his hands flying up in the air. "What! What happened?"

Karen laughed and adjusted the volume. "It's okay. That's called the volume control button. You turn it up or down, depending on how loud you want the music."

"You have a lot of magic in your world."

He wasn't sure he liked a world with so much magic. Standing Deer started exploring other buttons. Some of the buttons he played with didn't appear to do anything. Trying to figure out what they did, he pushed the same buttons repeatedly. Karen cleared her throat as he moved her seat back and forth several times without realizing it.

Telling him to leave that one alone, she couldn't drive properly with him playing with that button. Raising his eyebrows with laughter in his eyes, he played with the button as he watched her move back and forth.

Then, he found the button for the windows. With a huge smile on his face he watched the window...down, up, down, up, down, up, down, over, and over again. He was like a two-year-old child discovering the world around him.

After he was tired of playing with the window, he found the switch for the trunk. Laughing, Karen pulled over to shut the trunk door. She couldn't stop laughing. People drove by looking at her as if she needed a straightjacket. She explained to him to leave that button alone, too. It was so funny watching a grown man playing with those buttons. They were new toys for him.

Note to self: the next vehicle will not have a center console with control buttons.

Standing Deer hadn't been paying attention to what was outside of the car. He hadn't realized they arrived downtown until Karen told him. He gaped, open-mouthed in astonishment at the amount of cars and people,

"The buildings touch the clouds!" Rubber necking, Standing Deer stared out the window. "So many people! All different kinds of people from many different lands." He continued to look around in awe and pointed to a group of people. "I see your people have slaves here, too. The Lakota don't have slaves. They believe all people should be free."

Puzzled by his remarks, "Slavery was abolished after the civil war. What makes you think we have slaves?"

"What is abolished?" Standing Deer asked.

"It means stopped, forbidden. It is no longer legal to buy, sell, or own slaves."

"Then, why do your people still paint them black? Did the paint not wash off? When did you find out the war ended? The last I heard, your people were still fighting the Great White War. When we left the village, it had not ended yet."

Karen was even more puzzled than before. "What do you mean? I don't understand your question about the slaves."

"The black people, the one's your people paint black, so you would know who the slaves are and who the free people are. If your people no longer have slaves because of the Great White War, then why do you still paint them black?"

Interesting observation, she could understand how the Indians would come to that conclusion. They paint themselves for war and hunting, etc. Hopefully, she can keep him distracted, and avoid her slip about the war ending.

"We didn't paint them black. Many of their ancestors were taken from another country called Africa."

As they drove around the lake, it was quiet as Standing Deer watched and absorbed everything that was happening.

"What is that they are riding on?"

"Those are bicycles. They are used for transportation, recreation, and exercise."

Standing Deer exclaimed, "A white soldier!" Pointing to where he saw the man, "Why is he here?" He reached instinctively for his bow and arrow. Blowing out a breath, he remembered she had convinced him to leave it at her lodge with his knife.

Karen turned to see a city policeman on a horse. Deciding they had seen enough of the city. She needed to show him some of the farmland and orange groves.

"That is a policeman. He is here to protect the honest people from the dishonest people, like a dog soldier does. Let's get out of the city and go to more pleasant areas of this town."

Karen drove onto the east-west expressway and headed west. Standing Deer was ecstatic, exhilarated from the speed of the car. He turned the volume up on the radio and made whooping noises. Now he reminded her of a teenager, changing the radio to a rock station.

Standing Deer was moving his head and tapping his hand on his leg to the beat of the music. The song was unfamiliar to her. After the song was over, the DJ announced that it was Offspring.

"Did you like that song, Standing Deer?"

"I didn't understand the words but the music was great!"

Laughing, she didn't understand the words either.

He changed the radio station again, found country music, and decided to listen to that for a while. Then, he switched it to an oldie but goodies station where he left it. He increased the volume of the radio to listen to a Beach Boys song. Standing Deer figured out the radio pretty quickly.

The rest of the day flew by. She felt the more they spent time together, the more she realized how much she really liked and enjoyed his company. Though they were from two separate worlds, they had so much in common. Each moment seemed to bring Standing Deer more and more into her heart. The more they spoke of each other's feelings and dreams, the more she realized that he was the man for her.

By the end of the day, Karen knew in her heart that when she felt secure again, she would want to make love with him. Explaining to Standing Deer that she needed to go into the store and pick up a few things, she would be right out. He waited patiently, listening to the oldies station while she ran into the drug store.

Walking into the store, she didn't see her ex-boyfriend, David, in line at the checkout counter. She picked up a basket and walked straight over to the prophylactics. Grabbing a box, she heard an old familiar voice behind her.

"Well, I see you haven't changed, still so very practical. How come your boyfriend isn't buying those instead of you?" Smirking, "You never bought them for me."

"Not out chasing ambulances today, David?"

He growled. "I'm not an ambulance chaser."

"No, of course not. You just wanted me to hand out your business cards to my patients in the emergency ward for you. But when I refused, you convinced your other girlfriend to do it for you. You know the one you were cheating on me with? Or have you forgotten about her after she was fired for doing your dirty work? You realize that she can never be a nurse anywhere in this state because of you? You ruined her career to excel yours."

He retorted, "I didn't force her into doing anything." With his usual air of arrogance, the wrestler grin on his face, "I just got out of court. I won, as usual. So..."

"That's because you won't take it to court unless you know you'll win."

David ignored her and took the box of condoms from her. Twirling them around in his hand, he smiled. "Plan on having fun tonight?"

"Go to hell, David." She said quietly and walked away, leaving him holding the box of prophylactics.

"Whoa! Straight laced, goody two-shoes Karen said a naughty word!" David laughed as she walked away to pick up some other necessities.

With anger, jealousy, and resentment in his heart, David watched her walk away. Cautiously he started searching for a pin. He found a large button with a pin on the back. Carefully, he pulled out the wrapped condoms and methodically put holes in every single one. Then, he walked over to her. He would pay her back for leaving him. Smiling to himself, he would win her back, too.

David threw the box into the basket she was carrying. "Here, you forgot these." Saluting, "Have fun." He turned and walked out the door.

Karen was fuming at David's arrogance. How could she have ever seen anything in him? She hurried into line. He knew what her car looked like. Hopefully, he wouldn't go searching for it and find Standing Deer. That was all she needed, a confrontation between the two of them. He would humble

David. That was certain. David had no idea what he was up against. Thank God, he didn't have his knife with him.

Of all the people to bump into, it had to be him. How in the world she had ever gotten mixed up in that relationship she'll never know. She recalled Bonnie had told her it was hormones.

Karen's car was easy to find and David approached Standing Deer. "Whoa, ho, ho, ho." He mumbled. This was a classic rebound, definitely out of character. He never knew her to date men with dark hair, had always dated blondes. It was long, too, interesting, she always liked short hair on men.

"Hello. I'm an old, close friend of Karen's. Name's David." David reached his hand through the window to shake hands. Standing Deer just looked at it and silently looked at David, waiting for him to continue speaking.

Clearing his throat, uncomfortable with the rejection of the handshake, he was unaccustomed to rejection from anyone. It never happened, everyone liked him.

"Why don't you come out of the car? It must be hot in there. Karen will be out in a few moments." David opened the door and Standing Deer got out of the car.

"So..." David cleared his throat, trying to identify the accent. "How long have you known Karen?"

"I have not counted the days."

"Days?" She had only known him for days and is planning on going to bed with him.

Leaning against the parked car, accessing, planning, David scrutinized the man in front of him who was not very talkative, and quite stoic. This new beau of Karen's was quite tall, at least five inches taller than him, probably with some Native American blood in him, too. He felt he was the better man compared to this loser boy she was seeing now. The relationship wouldn't last, no competition between the two of them.

"Well, aren't you the lucky one. You have known Karen for days and she is willing to go to bed with you. She dated me for well over six months before she went to bed with me. Don't get your hopes up too high on having her for long. I will win her back."

Hurrying through the exit, she saw the two men talking by her car. David saw her coming up to the two of them and continued talking to Standing Deer.

"You may have her, now," David said quietly to Standing Deer. "But she will be my wife. Soon you will be out of her life and she will marry me." David turned and walked away.

Before David got into his car to drive away, he yelled to Karen. "Have fun, Karen!" Laughing as he drove off.

"What did he say to you?" Karen demanded.

"I don't like him. What he says doesn't matter. He is wrong and speaks like a foolish child."

Chuckling, "Well, I see you figured him out pretty quickly. I wish I had. Let's go."

When Karen saw the two of them together, there seemed to have been no comparison. Standing Deer had it all, compared to David. David was a scumbag, an ambulance-chasing lawyer, and a two-faced cheating liar.

Standing Deer had killed men without remorse. David hadn't. She didn't feel remorse over the death of those traders either. He was from a different world. Survival of the fittest...isn't that how it was supposed to be? She wasn't that blind to Standing Deer. Karen knew he could be a deadly, fierce warrior.

Even though she had only known Standing Deer for two weeks, she could see the major difference between the two men. Her relationship with Standing Deer was moving too fast. She had only known him a short time, but it seemed like it had been forever, like they were meant to be.

Since the first time he touched her, nothing was the same. She couldn't get him off her mind. It was as if something out there was telling her they were to be together until the end of time.

Sometimes love turns out that way. Could it actually be happening to her? Could Standing Deer be her soul mate? He seemed to be so perfect for her but...how would she really know if he was the right one?

She hadn't even gone beyond the ninety day infatuation period yet where gradually the real person starts coming out, unable to keep up the pretense of best behavior. Once that happens, it's a decision if you can live with their faults or not.

When she looked back on the past year, she realized she had been searching, looking for something beyond her reach. She was an independent, well-rounded person, yet it always felt as if something was missing, incomplete. Was Standing Deer the missing piece in her puzzle called life?

Why was she even considering these questions? She had not known him long enough. There were too many conflicts they had to encounter if they were to pursue this relationship. There was too much standing in their way. Then again, smiling, she always did enjoy a challenge.

Karen's train of thought was broken by the sound of the radio. Bouncing to the rhythm, Standing Deer turned up the volume. It appeared he liked The Beatles, too.

"Are you going to tell me what David said?"

Standing Deer shook his head. "The man is a child, lying to himself. He believes you will marry him." He grunted. She was the woman for Standing Deer. "He is a pampered white man." Standing Deer took an instant dislike to him. "There's something about the man I find hard to trust. He was too pleasant, at first, too talkative. It made me feel like he was hiding something." The white man appeared to be overconfident, like a child that feels as if they are indestructible.

"Wow, Standing Deer, it took me a year to see that."

Standing Deer shook his head. Her old friend David wasn't a strong enough man for Karen. "He needed you for your strength."

Karen knew Standing Deer didn't need her. He had his own inner strength. He didn't need it from anyone else.

"You are no longer friends?" Standing Deer recalled the look of dislike on Karen's face when she had approached the two men.

"Goodness, no."

He smiled, "he cannot win your heart? He would be able to give you more magic from your world that I cannot. He would not give himself, something you need and deserve." Standing Deer would give her his all, more than the other man would ever give her.

"He will never have my heart again and if there is something I want, then I can buy it myself. I don't need anyone's money."

When they arrived home, she went into the kitchen to prepare dinner. Standing Deer followed her in and offered his help.

As she reached around him to turn on the light, he softly touched her face. "It was a good day, Karen."

She smiled flicking the switch, "I really enjoyed myself, too. I hope the city didn't intimidate you or discourage you."

Standing Deer watched Karen turn the light on and was surprised by the burst of light in the room. He flipped the switch back and forth and watched the light turn on and off.

"What is intimidate?" He asked as he was playing with the light switch watching the light on the ceiling turn off and on. It was more interesting than the disappearing water from what she called a toilet.

"It means threatened or to make you feel threatened by the extensiveness of something."

He continued to switch the light on and off, trying to figure out how it worked, snorting. "No, it didn't make me feel threatened. We are all very small children in the eyes of the Great Spirit. It is just another world that he has given to his people. It is another world to learn about and discover."

Karen was just about to tell him to leave the light switch alone when he stopped. He walked around her to the stovetop, looking at the red coil underneath the pan. Removing the pan from the element, he put his hand over the top to feel the heat.

"What an odd fire. This is where you make you meals?"

"Yes, it's called a stove. It's an electric element. Don't touch it, it will burn you."

Standing Deer tilted his head and smiled. "If there is heat, there is usually fire. Where there is fire, one doesn't touch it unless one wants to be burned."

Of course he had common sense. He would need plenty of it to survive in the wilderness.

"Sorry," she apologized.

The evening continued with Standing Deer discovering new toys to play with, each room bringing him closer and closer to her world.

She grabbed the remote and turned on the news. He sat on the couch with eyes wide with astonishment. Standing slowly and with caution, walked to the television, looked underneath it and behind it. He rocked it, put his ear to it, and tapped it lightly with his finger.

Dumbfounded, he looked at Karen and then behind the television. "How do those tiny people get in there? Do they live in there?"

"No they don't live in there. It's called a television. It's like a picture, only it moves. They're people just like us only they're on the television." Karen paused unsure if she should continue the explanation. "It's a bit complicated. I don't think you would really understand, but I'll explain it to you if you would like. Actually, I find it hard to understand."

He sat down next to her. "No, that is all right. I have seen too much magic today. I don't think I want to know how it all works."

There was a small segment on the news about the senate and congress trying to pass a new bill taking some of the Native American Indian's privileges away. It would be breaking several treaties from the past.

"I see the white man doesn't keep his word in your world, either." Standing Deer said dryly.

"If I were you, I wouldn't worry too much about it. It'll cause too much of an uproar. There are so many Native American sympathizers across the United States that a bill like that would cause too many problems among the Americans. Unfortunately, sometimes not enough people speak up. They're just being politicians and are trying to get away with anything they can."

He grunted.

She waited a moment to see if he would say something. When he didn't she continued. "You see, the politicians are making a big deal about the national deficit. They think that by cutting back, on what they call unnecessary spending, it will help get rid of the deficit. Usually, it's an election year thing."

"What is a deficit?" Standing Deer asked.

"It means debt. Our country owes people, themselves, or the World Bank. Whatever, we owe them money."

"You mean your world is poor? It no longer has any of the white man's money?"

Karen laughed, not at his question but at the reality of his question. "No. Our country isn't poor. Actually, we are one of the most profitable countries in the world. In my opinion, and quite a few people would disagree with me, the politicians don't want us to know what the country's assets are or the actual debt ratio. They don't want the people of the United States to know how much they're worth."

Karen sighed, she tried to keep her political views to herself, but it was so easy talking to Standing Deer. Maybe someday, as they grew closer together, they would have their political discussions. Now that would be an "adventure", as Bonnie would say.

The news became a blur as Standing Deer cupped her face into his hands, leaning over to kiss her quickly and lightly on the lips. Looking deep into her eyes, penetrating his gaze into her being, he licked his lips.

Kissing and caressing her neck Standing Deer whispered. "My beautiful Karen, where shall we sleep tonight?"

"You dear, will be sleeping in the spare bedroom. I will sleep on the fold-out couch in the den."

"Why can we not sleep together? I want to hold you all night. We can sleep together without making love." His voice resonated with passion, "I want to make love to you only when you are ready."

That would be nice. She leaned toward him and closed her eyes, wanting the kiss he was about to give her.

He grinned, touching his lips gently to hers. The rush of the electrical impulse was intense. They both could feel their bodies reaching for each other, their desire immense.

Standing Deer wanted to lose himself in her arms. Not since his wife had he felt such a desire for a woman. He wanted to be with Karen for eternity. Feeling her energy, her soul, he wanted to be a part of it.

The intensity of the kisses grew stronger, his hands stroking her until she could only feel the heat from his touch. The more he kissed her, the more she wanted to kiss him back, not wanting to leave his embrace. This time she wouldn't walk away, knowing there wasn't anything wrong with just kissing.

Her heart pounded with desire. She felt him lifting her shirt. She arched her back as she felt his hot, moist mouth covering the nipple of her voluptuous breast. She ached for more as his lips went lower, slowly down to her waist. He tickled her belly button with a few flicks of his tongue.

Overcome with desire, a tiny voice inside said, "No, stop now before it is too late." She couldn't, didn't want to stop.

Standing Deer played with her nipples as he caressed her with his tongue. Karen froze, the attempted rape suddenly fresh in her mind.

Instantly he felt her discomfort. Not wanting to upset her, he moved his way upward. He just wanted to simply please her any way he could.

As he continued to caress her breasts, she started relaxing again, and felt on fire at the same time. His hands burned her flesh with desire, she could feel his fingers moving slowly...slowly down to her...she moaned in pleasure.

Standing Deer felt her swelling with his fingertips. She was ready for him, moist and hot. He had made her forget temporarily, knew her desire for him was ultimate, and probably wouldn't stop him if he tried to enter her. He gave his word and would keep it. He could feel her fighting it and knew he had to get her trust before she had her release.

Was that moan from him or her? As he stroked her gently, unfulfilled desires exploded from her being. She was burning...on fire. Time froze with the flames of desire engulfing her as her body quivered.

All thoughts ceased as time stood still. She felt a strange heated, burning sensation. The intensity claimed her, allowing him to have what no one else had given her. She felt a pulse; an exertion from inner release as her body exploded and shuddered. She gently returned exhausted from the intensity of the love.

Leaning his head on her chest, he could feel and hear her heart beat. "My love," he said huskily.

Karen started laughing, a giggly euphoria had taken control of her. It was silly but she was so happy she couldn't help it.

"Oh, that was oh so wonderful! I've never had an orgasm before. That was so...so...thank you. Never in my life have I experienced such intensity." Still out of breath, she continued. "You are wonderful, Standing Deer. Thank you."

Leaning back, still breathing heavily, he smiled, happy that he had pleased her. It's all he wished for at this time.

It was there that they both awoke the next morning, entwined in each other's arms...unknowingly, wrapping themselves around and into each other's soul.

Chapter Ten

At times throughout the day, Standing Deer was like a child discovering a whole new world. Their friendship grew strong as each spoke of their own lifestyles and experiences. Karen felt the bolt of electricity rush through her each time he gently touched her arm or held her hand.

They were developing a friendship she was unaccustomed to having with a man. She spoke with him of things that only she or her closest friends knew. Karen believed she could tell him almost anything and trusted him enough to know he wouldn't betray her. Maybe someday she would be able to entrust him with her biggest secret, the truth behind their separate worlds.

She was pleased when Standing Deer spoke about the ways of his people. He had seen on the news that a parent had been arrested for abusing and neglecting their children. Appalled at the notion, he told her the Indians from his tribe believed that it brought great shame and dishonor to your name if you ever hit any child in anger or for punishment. There was a communal effort, everyone considered themselves parents to all the children in the camp and believed it was everyone's responsibility to teach the children to grow to be brave and honest adults. They looked after each other, young and old.

She asked him what they did to Indians who had hurt their children. He told her it just didn't happen. No one wanted to live a life with dishonor clouding their lives.

He spoke of a father, from a different tribe who had been excessively beating his wife and children. The Indian was expelled from the life of the village and was told never to return. The wife was given the choice to stay or go; she chose to stay.

"Your people have divorce?"

"What is divorce?"

After she explained the meaning and concept of divorce, he responded. "One discourages divorce, although, it isn't forbidden. Depending on the circumstances, it can also be a dishonor. A warrior never tells his wife to leave, it is a lifelong vow. If she is unhappy with him, she may leave. It is so rare that I have never seen it happen. If he is unhappy with her, if he so chooses, then he takes another wife." Putting his hand in the air, "However, taking another wife doesn't necessarily mean he is dissatisfied with the first wife, either."

"Can a woman have more than one husband?"

"No."

"Why not?" Indignant with the negative answer, "that's not fair. If a warrior can have more than one wife why can't the woman choose to have more than one husband?"

Shaking his head, he laughed. "That isn't the way. Besides, there are more women than men. You, my love, are trying to be difficult."

He bent and gave her a kiss that sent her reeling in pleasure. She couldn't concentrate when he was kissing her with such seeded passion, arousing her so deeply, distracting her.

"The Sioux believe a wife is his equal and should always be treated with the love and respect she deserves."

He wouldn't be very impressed with her world if he knew about the divorce rate and abuse received by adults and children alike. He would be disgusted with all the rapes, murders, and robberies that happened daily. Iniquities her world seemed to take for granted. She was impressed with their beliefs regarding marriage and children. They were the ones that were considered savages but after listening to Standing Deer, were they really?

His life couldn't be that peaceful, could it? It sounded almost like paradise. Could their village be that serene? She recalled the happiness and serenity she had felt when she was with the Lakota. Their village may be peaceful and serene but what about their warfare with other Indian tribes? They fought, killed, and stole from other tribes, the white pioneers. She diplomatically worded the questions, hoping she didn't offend him.

"We are a peaceful people, we fight only when we are forced into it. We don't have warfare among ourselves. Our life-circles in the village remain at peace with each other."

"You fight and kill the Pawnee and other enemies of the Sioux. You steal their horses and anything you can from them in order to achieve coups. How can you say you are a peaceful people?"

"Doesn't your country award your people with honor for defeating an enemy? Do they not receive coups for conquering their enemies, stealing their possessions? Sioux don't war with Sioux. Americans kill Americans. We aren't like your people who kill each other for land and the white man's money. I have seen how your people treat each other, your country will not live as long as the Sioux Nation if they don't find peace amongst themselves."

Her mouth dropped, furious at his attitude. "How dare you! How can you say that when you war with your Indian enemies? Your people have fought the Pawnee for generations."

Standing Deer sighed. He didn't want to argue with her. "The Scili, the Pawnee Nation is our enemy. We don't provoke war with them. We aren't the same as the white man."

"You are still fighting among yourselves. Pawnee against Lakota is still Indian fighting Indian."

"Pawnee isn't Lakota. We aren't the same."

"You are the same! You're still Native Americans fighting against Native American's."

"I don't know how to explain this to you. They aren't the Sioux Nation. They aren't of the people. You are putting the Nations together in one bowl. You can't do that."

They were going in circles. "Standing Deer, some day you will have to join forces with all Indian Nations or your people will not survive."

"I will listen and heed your words for they are spoken with your heart."

Taking her into his arms, he gently kissed her lips, disarming her anger. Karen would treasure every moment in his arms, knowing that even if it was almost paradise, it wouldn't last for long. It saddened her to know that turmoil would soon surround and destroy the Indian lifestyle.

Before they both realized it, the day was over and they had returned to the Hunkpapa village.

"You must never speak of my world and what you have seen in it. It wouldn't be wise." She whispered to him as they left his lodge.

Shaking his head, laughing. "Little one, no one would believe me. They would think I had been drinking the white man's spirits."

The ceremonies had ended but there were many people from other bands still in the camp. Karen could see Crazy Horse and Red Cloud across the village. She would need to speak to him before he returned to his home.

"My friends!" Two Feathers called. Both Standing Deer and Karen watched Two Feathers approach with his customary smile on his face with Laughing Flower not far behind.

After a short spell, the men went on their way and the two women started their chores. Karen was clumsily trying to soften an antelope hide when she was approached by Sitting Bull, Crazy Horse, and Red Cloud.

"My father would like you to come to his lodge as soon as you can. He would like to speak with you before the big meeting of the chiefs," said Sitting Bull.

Karen immediately dropped what she was doing and walked over to Jumping Bull's lodge. As Sitting Bull opened the flap to let her inside her heart jumped. She felt a crushing sadness strike her hard in the face. She looked into Jumping Bull's eyes as he sat quietly and knew that Crazy Horse told of his experience in the Sun Dance. But what and how much did Crazy Horse know?

Sitting where she was instructed, she remained silent...waiting, fearing what the questions could possibly be. She looked over at Crazy Horse. He was so young, possibly fourteen or fifteen. He had the look of a man with years of wisdom. She could see his eccentricities in him even now. She reflected, a quiet boy/man with the weight of the world on his shoulders.

His wavy hair was braided on one side with a feather tying it back, his eyes a coal black, deep, and sullen. It appeared as if he looked straight through you. His build was lean and solid as a rock. It seemed odd but his skin was light, like hers. She hadn't noticed that earlier. The tension laid like a thick blanket hovering over them. Crazy Horse stared at her with conflicting emotions of concern and anger.

She turned her gaze to the famous Red Cloud. He had a kind face. He could be a fierce warrior, if one crossed him. Smiling, she was proud to meet such a great and honorable man.

Jumping Bull cleared his throat and started speaking in Lakota. Sitting Bull, who had seated himself between Jumping Bull and Karen, spoke quietly in her ear, interpreting.

"We are here to find answers to puzzling questions that have arisen in the past few days. Crazy Horse has seen a great and tragic vision. He says you know what the future will be and you can save us but you cannot. He says the Great Spirit will not allow Spirit of the Mountain to change what is to be. If you try, you will lose all of your powers that he has given you."

Jumping Bull put both hands on his crossed knees. "He didn't know where we had met and in the vision you were called Spirit of the Mountain. That will be your name from this day forward. Crazy Horse will speak now."

She turned her gaze to Crazy Horse. His head was down, his body so still that he appeared to be asleep. Inhaling a deep breath, he looked up, staring with hard, angry eyes. With resentment in his voice, he spoke quietly while Sitting Bull continued to translate.

"I have already given you the message from the Great Spirit. There is no need to repeat it. Now, I have been advised to tell you my vision. I will tell you, only because you are the link to our future." Crazy Horse paused and was silent for a few moments.

"There are white men and black slaves in our Sacred Hills. They are digging for the shiny rocks that the white men feel is so important. They are destroying our Sacred Grounds looking for these silly rocks. There is war, with many dead white and many dead, brave and honorable warriors.

I look to where the sun rises and I see many white people and families coming into our lands. They kill all our buffalo and we cannot eat or live." Crazy Horse looked to Red Cloud. Red Cloud nodded his head in encouragement and Crazy Horse continued.

"I see clouds and smoke everywhere. I cannot see the sky. There are many, many white soldiers and they have come to destroy us. They have come to our village to kill us all. They want to kill the women and the children as well as our warriors. During the fighting, you are there in the middle of the camp. You are helping the wounded warriors. There is a white glow like a full moon surrounding you. I'm ten feet from you and there is a white soldier on his horse racing toward you with his rifle aimed at your back. When I raise my rifle to shoot him I hear a whooshing sound like that of a thousand eagles flying over my head. The soldier's horse jumps up on his hind legs and knocks the white soldier onto the ground. The white soldier gets up and grabs his gun to shoot you when some unseen force pushes him down. The whooshing sound continues until I shoot the man." Crazy Horse shook his head in wonder, puzzled by the vision.

"You don't see what is happening. You are tending to a warrior and your eyes are turned away from the soldier. Women are grabbing you and taking you to wounded children and men alike for you to save them. The white glow, like a spirit, follows you. When the clouds and smoke are gone, you cry for the dead white men that are in our village." He cleared his throat and continued, allowing Sitting Bull the time he needed to repeat his words.

"There is a white man in the village that isn't dead and you go to him to try and save him. A warrior stops you and kills him. He tells you that we will take no captives. You walk away from the dead man." Crazy Horse looked at her with hardened, angry eyes. "That is when I received the message for you from the Great Spirit."

"Why did you try to save the white man? Your skin is white. Do you choose to be with the Lakota now? Then in the future when you feel as if all is lost, turn your back on the Lakota?"

Crazy Horse hissed at Karen. "I trust no one who is white. Why would the Great Spirit choose a white skin to help save the great Lakota Nation?"

Jumping Bull raised his hand and stopped the angry words coming out of Crazy Horse's mouth.

"Spirit of the Mountain, we are a peaceful people and don't want war. All we want to do is live on our land, raise our children with the freedom that our forefathers have given us, teach them the ways of the Great Spirit. Will the white soldier's not stop until we are all dead? How many will come to our lands?" Jumping Bull asked quietly.

Karen's head was throbbing, absorbing everything Crazy Horse had said to her. She understood why he was an eccentric, withdrawn man. He had the gift of sight and knowledge and he was going to fight this all the way. Red Cloud, Sitting Bull, and Jumping Bull waited patiently for her answer. Crazy Horse stared at her as if he knew what she was going to say before she said it. She could feel the anger bubbling inside of him.

Karen spoke slowly and cautiously, afraid she would say too much. "Even though I have the knowledge of what the future is supposed to be for your people, I cannot tell you what to do. I cannot tell you how to prevent the tragedies that will happen."

She paused, her heart pounding in her ears, she wiped her sweaty hands on her dress. "All I can tell you is to try your best for peace. Once the Civil War is over there isn't much anyone can do to stop the white immigrants from coming onto your land. There are thousands and thousands of whites that will be coming to this land to start new lives. Almost all of them will fear you and your ways. They don't understand the Indian's way of life and have been told that you are uncivilized savages. They have been told you will kill them on sight and must defend themselves because you will hurt their wives and children."

Taking a drink from her cup, she tried to figure out how to word everything carefully. "Most of these people are poor and want to live in peace as you do and want to start a new life. If we could all live in peace and harmony, there would be no destruction."

Karen looked directly at Crazy Horse. "Not all whites are evil, most are hardworking, brave, and honest."

"They will take what doesn't belong to them! You know there will be no peace!" Crazy Horse shouted at her.

"I can't deny what you say. Don't be angry with me because of what has happened. I can't change..." Immediately her anger and frustration had become dread. She had spoken in the past tense!

She looked around quickly and saw the astonishment in everyone's faces, everyone except for Crazy Horse who couldn't understand English.

"Why do you speak as if this is the past?" Red Cloud questioned.

A sick feeling grew into a knot in Karen's stomach; her heart stuck in her throat. "I know too much. It is hard for me not to warn you of what is to be. I cannot tell you anything else."

There was a short silence when Jumping Bull dismissed Karen and Crazy Horse. The men prepared for their meeting with the other chiefs. There was much to discuss as there had been rumors that the Great White War was almost over and white men had been seen digging for the rocks in *Paha Sapa*, the Sacred Black Hills.

Karen was relieved to be away from such scrutinizing questions.

Chapter Eleven

Karen had been waiting patiently for Standing Deer to return. Almost everyone she knew in the village had been teaching and helping her learn the language and ways of the Lakota. Sunshine in the Morning and Laughing Flower had taught her how to prepare foods and medicines. Karen wasn't familiar with the plants but found the herb medicines to be quite effective. The only plant she seemed to recognize was the mint plant they used for their tea.

Their English was limited. However, Sunshine in the Morning, proficient with sign, helped her when they spoke to her in Lakota. Karen wanted to surprise Standing Deer with what she had learned when he returned.

Karen listened to the elders as they told tales, teaching lessons and morals to the children. They used sign language as they spoke so she could understand and comprehend the stories. Many sounded like ones she had heard when she was younger, with symbolisms and deep meaning. The children would listen hard with their hearts so they wouldn't miss a word.

Living in the village and spending so much time with Sunshine in the Morning and Laughing Flower made her aware of how spiritual the Lakota were, praying each morning and at the end of each day. They would pray to the Great Spirit before a hunt, thank him for the kill, and the chance to feed those who were hungry; grateful for everything He had given them. They never wavered in their beliefs. Everything was as He wanted it to be and one must accept His complete wisdom and do as He bid.

The people of the tribe thought it was strange when Karen informed them that her people chose one day a week to go to church and pray to God. They did not put one day aside as a holy day to pray like the modern Christians. All days belonged to the Great Spirit, everything they did, and everything they owned. They couldn't understand how her people took just one day when all should be grateful to God each day; therefore, they should thank Him and praise Him always.

Always watching and learning, Karen observed the warriors who returned with a bountiful kill. If they had more than they needed, they would give the food to someone less fortunate. The people were careful in their generosity. It wasn't because they didn't want to give. They made sure their gifts never offended or made someone feel as if they weren't contributing their share. They took care of each other, young and old alike. Watching the way they lived increased Karen's spiritual beliefs in God. She felt it was ironic that she had to travel over a hundred years to find the inner peace she had been looking for all of her life.

She was quickly becoming a naturalist with a strong emotional attachment to God and everything He had given the Earth. The Lakota treated the land and all its creatures with reverence. They were all gifts from the Great Spirit and must be treated with respect; they didn't take any more than was needed.

On the morning of the warriors return, Karen and Sunshine in the Morning were filling their skins with water. Hearing the excitement from the village, they went to greet and welcome the men. Karen stood back as she watched Little Fox and Sunshine in the Morning hugging their brother. She scrutinized every square inch of his body to make sure he was unharmed and found herself becoming aroused. As she looked up into Standing Deer's eyes, he could see the spark of her desire.

Walking to her, he kissed her gently, sending the now familiar surge of power through both of their bodies. Smiling, he looked into her eyes with love. "I hear you have kept everyone busy with your never-ending thirst for knowledge."

Huskily Karen said in Lakota, "*Iyuskin kuwa, Tahina Nazinpi.*" I welcome you, Standing Deer.

His heart nearly burst with pride and happiness. Perhaps winning her love wouldn't be as hard as Bonnie said it would. He kissed her again.

Excusing himself, he explained that he had to meet with the warriors and entered Jumping Bull's lodge to inform their chief of what had conspired. She wasn't sure if she wanted to know, certain the law of the Lakota Nation had taken care of the gold-diggers.

After the evening meal, Standing Deer had asked Karen to walk with him. He was pensive and uncertain of how she would feel after he told her about the white men. He felt he needed to discuss it with her. Stopping in the privacy of the woods, she leaned against a tree anticipating and dreading the forthcoming conversation.

"I must tell you about the white men."

She nodded, encouraging his words. She didn't want to hear them, but understood that he needed to speak with her to ease his conscience.

"Our intentions were to tell the white men to leave and never return, but they opened fire. We had no choice but to defend ourselves. They had cornered themselves. There was no honor in this. It was a pitiful waste of lives." He sighed, looking at her with genuine sadness, hoping she wouldn't hate him. "We won't be giving the white man any more chances."

"You did what was necessary. It doesn't matter what their skin color was."

Sweeping her into his arms, his eyes flooded with the relief and desire, kissed her throat, face, and lips, whispering seductively in her ear. "*Wastehca.*"

Puzzled, Karen looked into his eyes. "*Wastehca?* I thought that meant delicious, as in food?"

Nuzzling his face into her neck, caressing her throat with his tongue, he laughed. "It does my love, and your kisses taste sweet and delicious. I will never be able to have enough of you."

He grabbed her closer and seized her being, attacking her emotions with excitement caused by the touch of his hands and lips. The electric pulse surged through her with each touch as her body naturally leaned closer into his, becoming one. They both felt the fires consume them and ignite a deep soaring passion.

Karen gave in to their desires and allowed herself to be swept away by the sweet rapture of his caresses. All conflicts were gone from her mind, she thought of only him and the pleasure and security she felt in his arms. They returned to Standing Deer's lodge after the long teasing sensuous walk by the water's edge. He had made Karen feel as if she was the most important person in the world. When they sat next to each other on the buffalo skin blanket, Karen's deerskin dress crept up to expose her muscular thighs.

Standing Deer could see her satin undergarment sensuously peeking out. Karen didn't miss his reaction and watched with an inner satisfaction as he grew hard and firm.

As she placed her hand on his thick, massive thigh, she leaned closer. Languorously, she reached over with her other hand and took his large hand into hers giving him a lingering, gentle kiss. She tasted the sweetness of his mouth. Licking her lips, she craved for more.

The electric impulse that she had avoided for so long was as strong as their first kiss. An emotional explosion of heat pounded and thrust through their bodies as they melted into one another's hot flesh. The kissing and caressing slowly became a heated passion experienced like no other.

"Do you have your protection that you feel is needed?" Standing Deer voice sounded husky with desire.

Karen nodded her head yes, wondering how she had gotten on her back. She was filled with fear, desire, and excitement of the anticipation of their lovemaking.

With trembling hands, slowly and sensuously Standing Deer began to take off the deerskin. Sliding his hands underneath her dress, he felt the satin lingerie. Standing Deer inhaled a deep breath. In the dim light of dusk, each languorous movement showed her shaped, muscular body under the translucent lingerie.

He kissed her deeply and intensely as he carefully laid her down onto the buffalo skin blanket. Standing Deer felt as if he was going to go crazy with desire for her, wanting to submerge and bury himself in her silk and satin covered body. His hands trembled with desire as he began to remove the undergarment.

Underneath her lingerie, Standing Deer kissed and caressed her silky, smooth skin. He closed his eyes reveling in the feel of her skin on his hot lips and the lingerie against his rough hands as he slid them off and tossed them to the side.

It was hard for him to tell the difference between the two. Her skin felt just as soft as her undergarment. His touch was a methodical and gentle caress as he cupped one of her voluptuous breasts in his hand and felt the nipple stand erect in his fingertips. Karen arched her back begging him to continue the overwhelming pulse of electric rapture.

He felt a rush of heat go through his lips as Karen moaned in pleasure and contentment. Slowly, Standing Deer placed his hot, moist lips onto her breasts and suckled them until her body stiffened from the heated desire she felt engulfing her very being. His hand moved across and down her flat, muscular stomach. She was ready. He closed his eyes and relished in the sweet, desirable scents of her body.

Standing Deer kissed her passionately and tasted the sweetness as Karen arched her back in ecstasy. They were alone in this world of pleasure, as time stood still their two souls ever entwining for eternity.

Standing Deer could feel her body tremors and quivers as she experienced the ecstasy of an orgasm. He held her tightly as her body trembled from the intensity of their lovemaking. Her heart raced. Her body felt as if it had weights holding her to the ground. She couldn't move and it felt wonderful. She smiled and lifted her arm slowly to hold him closer.

When her body allowed itself to be commanded, Karen started to kiss and caress his nipples. Standing Deer found the feeling to be erotic as every part of his body seemed to be electrified by her caresses. Gradually and unsure of herself, she moved her way downward.

She was more than happy to return and give any pleasure to him that she could. She wanted to excite and satisfy him as he did her, wanting to make him explode in sheer pleasure and ecstasy. Karen wanted to make him squirm with desire and have him reach a peak he had never experienced in his lifetime.

Cautiously and slowly she allowed her tongue to caress him, she felt self-conscious of her actions but it seemed to her, the slower she moved, the more intense it was for Standing Deer. The slower she caressed him with her mouth, the more his body bucked with pleasure. He moaned as he opened his eyes and watched her work her charms on him.

Karen could see the fire of lust and desire flooding from his eyes, encouraging her to continue pleasuring him.

The intensity was too much, Standing Deer felt as if he was about to explode when he stopped her. He couldn't take anymore and needed to be deep inside of her, engulfing her hot, soft body.

Karen leaned over and grabbed a package. Caressing his manhood, she opened it as he watched her with burning desire. Slowly, continuing with the intensity that neither had ever experienced, she slid the prophylactic on his engorged, trembling member. It was all he could take.

"Now?" Standing Deer croaked breathlessly.

Karen nodded her head yes, afraid to speak, afraid no sound would come out of her mouth.

Standing Deer rolled on top of her and slowly entered her. He felt a tightness engulf him and the moist heat surround him as he entered her. It took all of his control not to explode as he felt the softness of her body wrap and squeeze his member.

An animal lust overcame the two of them as their bodies became entwined. Submerged in each other's soul, oblivious to all around them, the rhythm of their lovemaking continued. Standing Deer and Karen could no longer contain their passions, no longer wanted to.

At the peak of all their wondrous love, Standing Deer exploded deep inside of her, feeling her soft womanhood caressing him with her own pulsations. His body jerked from the impact of release as Karen received his love and clung onto him in seeded passion.

The two of them lay together in an easy embrace for several minutes. Exhausted and completely satisfied, they were oblivious to the world around them, conscious only of each other. Possessively, they held each other, not wanting their private world destroyed by the hard realities of life.

Standing Deer kissed her face and neck, never wanting to let go, clinging to the continuous embrace.

"*Waste celake.*" I love you. He murmured lovingly.

Lost in his eyes, feeling complete love of a man for the first time, she whispered to him, "Forever."

After a few moments, Standing Deer leaned up on one elbow and removed the condom. Unbeknownst to him, it was torn. He didn't have the knowledge to look for issues and wouldn't know what it would look like if it was damaged. He just knew it was what Karen desired and he would follow her wishes.

He stared into her eyes and caressed her face with his fingertips. He traced along her eyes and down her nose, looking at the freckles scattered about. Grabbing a handful of her soft curly hair, untangling it with his fingers, he watched it shimmer in the light. It still amazed him that she had so many different colors in her hair.

Karen watched him as he played with the separate strands of hair. She hadn't realized how light her hair was until she saw it lying next to his. His hair was as black as a raven's and intermingled with hers made an interesting contrast. It was tickling her chest and she could feel a slight velvety softness caressing her breasts. It stirred her to desire and she could feel the flame within her being as she reached up and pulled his sweet lips to hers.

"Did I not satisfy you, my love?"

"Oh yes, you did." Karen grinned and rolled him over onto his back. "But I think we might need more practice."

A husky laugh escaped from Standing Deer as they again found themselves merging into each other's souls. Both knew their time together was precious, each moment cherished as if it might be their last. Karen had never felt so much love from any man. All these years she searched for such a love and now she had it deep in her soul. She had learned to have spiritual inner peace with God and found the love of a lifetime. Everything she had always wanted.

She believed the conflicts that the Sioux Nation would face were going to cause friction between her and Standing Deer, as well as other members of the tribe. Why did she have to find the perfect love here, in the past? She didn't want to lose Standing Deer but how would she live with the constant conflict of their people?

Every private moment they could steal was enflamed in a passion that nothing could extinguish. Their two separate energies had become one and each strengthened the other.

Both avoided the knowledge that the time would come when a decision had to be made. Standing Deer didn't care for Karen's world but he didn't want to live without her. Several times he mentioned joining in marriage and she had graciously and lovingly declined, coming up with more reasonable excuses than he would like to count.

She had given herself and lived with him as a wife does and the members of his tribe, as well as himself expected a marriage. She had not asked him to join her in her world and he wasn't going to ask to go with her. She must understand that in his world they live as man and wife. It is expected that they honor their marriage in a ceremony.

Her time with Standing Deer and the Lakota passed quickly. One more night and her friend Bonnie would remove the canopy and she would have to return to the modern world. Could she do it without Standing Deer knowing he was now a complete part of her? Not wanting to imagine what it was like to be without him at her side, she avoided the nagging fears of what was to be.

How would she tell Standing Deer? Was she a fool to allow herself to fall in love when she knew it was wrong? She had allowed her heart to guide her decision. It was going to hurt when she told him they couldn't be together. It was going to tear her apart.

When Sitting Bull had approached her, she knew something was amiss. She knew how religious the Lakota were. What made her think that they would make an exception to the rule? With her mouth open in astonishment, she listened to his words.

"What! I have to what?!" She exclaimed, horrified by the seriousness in Sitting Bull's tone.

"You and Standing Deer have lived as man and wife. We have been patient because you aren't completely familiar with the ways of our people. Standing Deer says that he has asked you to marry him and you said no. It is our way, you must marry."

Karen was furious, a shotgun wedding, only it was drastically reversed! No matter how much she argued with Sitting Bull, she was cornered and was to be married that day. Sitting Bull knew she would be leaving soon but not for good. For every argument she gave him, he came back quickly with a better one. Now she knew why he became such a famous diplomat.

In a huff, completely defeated, she stomped off in the direction of Standing Deer's lodge. She was going to tell him a thing or two.

She was quickly sidetracked by Sunshine in the Morning and Little Fox. They were to prepare her for the ceremony and she wasn't allowed to see Standing Deer until the prayers began.

Chapter Twelve

"*Hiya.* No. I will not be bullied into marriage. I don't want to commit myself to Standing Deer knowing that our happiness will be threatened every day. We will be living separate lives. A marriage cannot exist that way."

Karen looked at the dress spread out before her. It was Laughing Flower's wedding dress and it was beautiful. It was beaded intricately with rabbit fur sewn underneath the beads and along the sides. Next to the dress lay matching moccasins and a headdress adorned in the same manner.

Sunshine in the Morning frowned. She didn't understand why Spirit of the Mountain was so furious. Didn't she love her brother? She should be honored to have such a good warrior for a husband. She watched as Karen stood in the middle of the lodge with her arms crossed, refusing to budge.

"*He woniya tawa, len u wo...lehan*!" Jumping Bull's angry voice called to Karen. Spirit of the Mountain, come here...now.

Karen walked out of the lodge, determined not to waver from her refusal to marry. She didn't want to anger him. He was like a father to her. Karen sighed when she saw the look of anger in his eyes. She knew then that she would do what he asked.

"You my adopted daughter. I grow to love you as my own child. You know most ways of Lakota. Don't dishonor yourself. You aren't spoiled child and shouldn't act like spoiled child." Taking both of her shoulders into his hands, he kissed her on the cheek, nodded his head, and briskly turned her around as he walked her into the lodge. After a few moments, he left to prepare himself for the ceremony.

With a deep sigh, Karen allowed the two women to prepare her for the marriage ceremony with Standing Deer. They could hear the drums beating, alerting the tribe of the coming ritual.

Her stomach was in knots, her hands sweaty and shaking uncontrollably. What was Standing Deer doing? How did he feel, knowing that she had already told him she didn't want to marry? Why was he allowing this to happen when he knew how she felt? She asked Little Fox and Sunshine in the Morning as they were helping her pull the dress over her head.

"He wishes to marry you. But even he has no choice," Little Fox explained.

"The law of the Lakota must be kept by all." Sunshine in the Morning added as she placed the decorative headdress on Karen.

After a few minutes that felt like eternity, Jumping Bull called to enter. Little Fox and Sunshine in the Morning responded to his request.

Smiling, Little Fox spoke quietly to Karen. "It is time."

As Karen and Jumping Bull left the lodge, a silence swept through the village. All eyes were on the two of them as they walked slowly to the center of the village. Karen's heart was thumping so hard that she felt as if all would hear.

Sitting Bull stood in the center of the village waiting patiently. He was impressively attired in full headdress and ritual ropes for the marriage ceremony. The photographed images she had seen of him did him no justice. They failed to capture the real man; the love and pride he had for his people.

She was honored to know him and felt privileged for the honor of having him marry her to Standing Deer.

Marry her! What was she thinking? She couldn't marry him! There would be too many hardships. The marriage would fail miserably. She stopped suddenly, looking at Jumping Bull, pleading silently to stop the madness. He wasn't blind to her fears, but refused to allow her to face shame. He knew they loved each other and belonged together.

He whispered to Karen. "It is meant to be."

Inhaling deeply, trying to calm her nerves she scanned the people who had gathered to watch the ceremony. Out of the corner of her eyes, she could see Standing Deer and Two Feathers approaching Sitting Bull. They would meet in the middle, thus connecting and combining their life-circles so they would become one. Fear trickled away when she looked upon the warrior she loved. Maybe, just maybe, love would prevail.

The drums stopped. Sitting Bull started reciting the prayers in Lakota, he spoke first to the Great Spirit and then spoke of what was expected of them as a couple.

She understood some of the words. It didn't matter. From the moment they joined each other in front of Sitting Bull, Karen was swept up and captured in the depth of Standing Deer's eyes. As the gentle words rested upon her heart it felt cleansed of worry. They could make it work.

Tearing herself from the link of love with Standing Deer, she blinked, dazed as she looked over to Sitting Bull. Did he say something? She looked around and saw everyone staring at her, waiting.

Sitting Bull raised his eyebrow and repeated in Lakota, then in English. "Do you accept these vows?"

"*Sha.*" Yes.

"Standing Deer, do you accept these vows?"

"*Sha.*"

Sitting Bull continued with his prayers to the Great Spirit, asking for the union to be blessed and their future to be guided by Him.

The circle waited.

When he didn't respond, Sitting Bull nudged him. "Standing Deer, the moment is here to seal your vows."

Standing Deer concluded his part of the sacred ceremony as was custom with the Lakota beliefs when he took a wife. When he was finished Karen smiled up at the man who was now her husband. As was customary with her beliefs, she grabbed both sides of his face and pulled him toward her. As their lips touched, the fire surged, penetrating their hearts and souls, etching a permanent flame of love and commitment that would burn forever.

Smiles brightened both of their faces.

A loud cheer filled the air and the after ceremony celebration began with dancing and a multitude of food, ending late into the night.

Karen and Standing Deer were exhausted from the excitement of the day. As they entered his lodge, she teased him that he had tricked her into marrying him and never thought she would see the day when she would be involved personally in a shotgun wedding. He feigned injury to his heart and strode over to her in one sleek and graceful movement.

"*Niye mitawa.*" You are mine.

With care, he removed the beads and feathers in her hair and loosened the curls to fall down upon her shoulders. He kissed and caressed her and then with a surge of intense heat claimed her lips. They caressed with their hands and lips, each seeking to increase the feverish heat that was sweeping through their souls.

Untying her dress, it dropped to the floor. Surprised to find she had worn nothing of the white women's undergarments, he was pleased and disappointed. Pleased she would choose to dress in the way of the Indian and disappointed because he liked the soft touch of the lingerie. It gave him more to seek pleasure with.

A deep sensual laugh came from within as he placed his mouth on her breasts. They peeked quickly with his touch and gave him the satisfaction that she desired him as much as he had her. Karen was fumbling with his breeches, frustration stifling her fingers as she tried to free him.

Standing Deer chuckled again. "Patience, my love, we have all night."

He proceeded to aid her in the disposal of his clothing, torturing her with his sweet caresses. The pleasure painfully sweet, she felt her knees weakening. Standing Deer's strong arm held her tight and securely. Tonight, she would fly with the stars into the heavens. He would make sure of it.

Keeping that promise he had made to himself, both soared to the heavens, following a path that pulsed through the ever eternal beating of the universe.

Karen wanted more, wanted to give as much as she received. She briefly wondered why she had never felt this way before, only with Standing Deer. The thought was gone as quickly as it came. Nothing mattered at that moment except the mad desire to have him. There was nothing but Standing Deer as she felt him against her.

She was with him. And she was in the heavens.

They moved sensually with the rhythm of the universe, their skin, and beings on fire from the bursting flames of passion. Karen didn't know when it happened but somehow she was laying down, pulling on his hair. Shivering from the touches of his tongue, he was sensually attacking her. He was everywhere, touching...feeling...caressing.

The intense sensations of pleasure pulsed through her body and she tightened in the burst of an orgasm. She started to scream from the pleasure and Standing Deer thrust his mouth hard onto hers to stifle the sounds. He moved his throbbing manhood, rubbing it alongside her inner thighs, and along the peak of her womanhood. She ached to have him inside of her, eyes full of lust and desire.

She begged him, whimpering. "Please. Oh please, I want you inside of me, deep inside of me."

"Not yet, I shall torture you with complete love so you will never forget me, no matter which world you are in."

He continued the torturous pleasure, a world unknown to her. A fever had consumed her, the only thing she wanted and cared about was to have him...now.

With all her might, consumed by the fires surrounding and engulfing them, Karen turned Standing Deer and pushed him flat onto his back. She reached for his manhood and was placing it in her when he forced her to stop, just barely remembering the promise he had made her.

"No, not yet."

Karen growled in frustration, tears filling her eyes as Standing Deer quickly placed the condom on his throbbing member, unknowingly tearing it in his own frustration to hurry.

"Now, please Standing Deer, now."

Quickly he plunged deep inside of her and heard the sound of satisfaction, the sounds of lust out of Karen's mouth, or was it his? He couldn't tell and didn't care as he thrust deeper, lost in the heat of the moment...lost in the heavens.

Sweet surrender came swiftly for they were both peeked and high from the sensations of the lovemaking. Collapsing from sheer exhaustion, their hearts were pounding. The sounds of the night creatures slowly came back to their senses, as if they were actually returning to earth.

Standing Deer heard her sniffle.

"Did I hurt you?"

"Oh no. Heavens no. I've just...I've never ever had...I've never felt this way before. I never knew it could be this beautiful."

"Then why do you cry?"

Karen laughed. "Because I'm happy. *Waste celake.*" I love you.

She kissed him, feeling his fire grow again. She laughed as she cupped his manhood in her hands, stroked him until he was ready to pleasure her again with his love. Slowly this time, he planned to make love and cause her senses to reel again, but ever so slowly.

When he had taken her to another explosive paradise, they fell asleep in each other's arms. Tomorrow they would think of reality.

And tomorrow came too quickly.

Scouts spotted Buffalo and half the village was preparing to leave by morning. She watched as the people readied themselves, amazing at the sight. In few short hours more than half the village was ready to go.

The next day she bid farewell to Standing Deer, wondering when she would see him next. Only having two more days before she had to start her new job, she wondered what was going on with Bonnie. What if the canopy wasn't working the way they believed and she was stuck here in this world? She shook her head, too many questions, not enough answers, and she would find out soon enough.

Reality set in the minute Karen awoke to the smell of brewing coffee. Standing Deer had gone on the buffalo hunt but Karen had still felt comfortable in the village. Now she was home and it was time to face the real world, her world. She smiled to herself, not that Standing Deer's world wasn't real; it would be nice if she actually was married to him. She would never be able to accept that marriage ceremony as a real marriage. She performed the ceremony to appease Jumping Bull and his people and no other reason. She certainly couldn't be held to it, in this world anyway.

She heard noises in the kitchen. Bonnie must be there waiting for her arrival. Stretching quickly, she jumped up and changed into modern clothing.

She had never expected to see Bonnie in such a state.

"What? What's wrong?"

Bonnie was in a frenzy.

It was obvious her friend needed to talk, the words spitting out of her mouth.

"That son of a...that jerk of a husband has been cheating on me for years."

An argument the night before finally brought on the confession from his lips. Bonnie finding him with the woman wasn't just a one-time thing. Then he took her car out of spite and left his. Of course, it had no gas and she had to walk to the gas station the next morning.

It was bad enough that she had to wait an extra night to take care of the canopy. That was the fateful night she found her husband in their bed with that woman. Have they no shame?

He actually had the audacity to ask her what she was doing home. Then that woman made a smart remark about her being scatter-brained and maybe she couldn't remember where she should be.

Never in her life had she ever attacked anyone with so much anger and vengeance. Her husband had to pull her off the woman and hold her against the wall while his mistress dressed herself and left.

Her world was destroyed. She had never felt so much hatred toward anyone.

"I knew you would be worried. I tried to get here as soon as I could." Bursting into tears, "Can I stay for a few days until things calm down?"

Karen cradled her closest friend in her arms. Bonnie and Kevin are getting a divorce? No way! They had the perfect marriage. What was he thinking when he took that other woman into his arms?

"What am I going to do?" Bonnie whimpered. "My life is over. I feel so stupid and blind. How am I supposed to counsel married couples when I can't even keep my own husband out of someone else's bed?"

"Bonnie stop, you're being unreasonably cruel to yourself. You are far from stupid and blind. He was your husband. Trust comes with that love. Are you sure you want to divorce him?"

"Oh yes, I'm sure." She growled in anger, walking over to the tissue box for a tissue. "I probably could forgive him if it was just a one-time fling, but he's been seeing her for years, almost four years. My God Karen, he'd been with another woman for four years. I didn't even see it. Can I stay here for a while? I won't be in the way. I promise. And if I get on your nerves just tell me."

"Of course you can stay here. As long as you want or need to. Now let me get that cup of coffee I so desperately need."

They talked for a couple of hours before Bonnie had to rush off for an appointment. With Bonnie's help, Karen caught up on everything that had, of course, fallen behind in her absence. When Karen got to the part of the marriage ceremony and her attitude that it wasn't a real marriage, Bonnie was dismayed.

"What do you mean it isn't a real marriage?"

"Well, how can you take a marriage seriously that supposedly happened over a hundred and thirty years ago, performed by a Lakota holy man and not in a church? Be serious, I love Standing Deer but marriage is out of the question. We've only known each other a month. I only did it to make Jumping Bull happy. It is their way and if I'm going to be living among them or in that time then I have to live by their rules. It was nice living in a fantasy temporarily. They're certainly not the rules that I have to live by here."

"You are rationalizing. Karen, you are married under the eyes of God, regardless of what priest or religious ceremony was performed. You are

Standing Deer's wife whether you like it or not. You'll just have to have a ceremony here in order for it to be accepted in this world."

She was angry by her friend's attitude. "I don't think so, Bonnie."

"You don't have a choice. You are married under the eyes of God. You are married to Standing Deer. Will he be coming to live here? Have you decided or have the two of you not even discussed it?"

Speaking through clenched teeth, "I don't know and we aren't married."

She caught the familiar strain in Karen's voice. She was pushing her too hard, too fast. Quickly deflecting, Bonnie brought up the new job.

Relieved, Karen was more than happy to change the subject.

Chapter Thirteen

The past two months had been exhausting and exciting. Her job had kept her considerably busier than she had anticipated. Bonnie's life was in shambles, and she hadn't seen Standing Deer in months. Every time he came back from a hunt; he was sent off to the Black Hills to do more fighting.

She had slept in the spare bedroom several times and intentionally missed him in between travels. She realized now, how much he meant to her. Were they really married? She recalled her feelings after the ceremony, and her adamant denial to Bonnie. At the time, she was still angry with him for forcing her to marry, to do the sacred marriage ceremony. She should be determined to make her marriage work. When she came back to the modern world and it all seemed unreal.

A deep lump stuck in her throat. She had missed him so much it hurt.

It had been easy avoiding the village but as time passed by, it was getting harder. She was determined to return and settle their life, and decide how they planned to live it. The time of uncertainty was over.

Her heart raced from the excitement of her marriage, the confusing and conflicting feelings of being married and not being married. In his world, his beliefs, they were husband and wife. To her, they weren't. It wasn't done by a priest, or minister, no papers were signed, no pre-nups. They really weren't married, no matter how much at times, she felt they were.

She wasn't the type of person to give up. Defeat never sat well with her. If they were to be married, she would fight for it, for him until the day she died.

She looked around at the sterile environment of the hospital emergency room. In approximately six months, she would be here at this hospital as a patient having Standing Deer's baby. Frustrated, she wondered how she became pregnant, then laughed at herself. She knew how, but still wondered how it could have happened. They had been so careful.

She heard someone call her name. She groaned as she watched her ex approach her.

"David, please don't call me Karen at work." She looked around feigning a puzzled look on her face. "I haven't heard an ambulance in the last few minutes. What are you doing here? Trying to hand out more business cards?"

Ignoring the sarcasm, he was confident her tune would change soon. "Excuse me, Dr. Anderson, but I have a client in intensive care. I was leaving when I saw your beautiful face."

Karen looked into his eyes and wondered what he wanted from her. She watched his face light up as he gave her his best charming smile.

"Let's go for some coffee." He said with a grin from ear to ear. "Then you can tell me everything that has been happening and when the baby is due."

"W—what did you say?" A knot was quickly developing in her stomach.

"Didn't Bonnie tell you I saw her the other day? I'm so excited for us. It's too bad your loser boyfriend hasn't been around for a few months. But that makes everything easier for us, doesn't it?"

"Us? What do you mean by us?"

She boiled inside as he continued talking, playing his game as he ignored her questions. She was quickly jolted back to what he was saying when he mentioned marriage.

"What did you just say?"

"Karen, Dr. Anderson, pay attention. This is important. I know you too well. You wouldn't be able to have an illegitimate child. It goes against everything that you believe in and all of your wonderful morals and principles."

Bonnie doesn't know. She couldn't know.

Gently taking her arm, he guided her toward the doctor's break room. "You know I can't have kids. This would be perfect. We can get married and I will raise the little munchkin as my own. It would be wonderful. I'll make you the happiest person in the world."

David was beaming with excitement and Karen felt as if she was going to be sick. An undeniable alarm and warning light went off in her head.

"How did you know I was pregnant?"

With the ease of the typical lawyer she felt he was, he lied with compassion.

"Why darling, Bonnie told me."

"I haven't told her." Karen stopped in the middle of the hallway.

"Well, then, she obviously guessed."

"No she didn't. She's had enough problems of her own and doesn't need to be worrying about me. I haven't told Bonnie. So David, tell me again. HOW did you know?"

"Don't you want to marry me and have this baby?" He asked her tenderly as he stroked the side of her arm. He reached up to trace the outside of her lips, getting uncomfortably close. "I love you. I want you to have this baby. That baby is mine. If it wasn't for me, you wouldn't be having it,"

"What do you mean if it wasn't for you I wouldn't be having it? What did you do, David?" Karen was almost growling.

"Oh baby. Darling, don't be mad. I did it for us. That man wasn't for you anyway, and I am. I couldn't give you a baby so I arranged it so he would give you what I couldn't." Excitement elevated his voice, "Now we can be together for the rest of our lives. I'll raise the child as my own because, I planned him. I planned the whole thing."

Karen's breath was coming faster and faster. Seething inside and about an inch from exploding right there in the middle of the hallway, she turned and quickly walked toward the break room knowing David would follow.

"How?" She asked through clenched teeth.

He smiled and shrugged. "I put holes in the condoms. Okay? How else was I going to get you pregnant? You wouldn't have gotten pregnant voluntarily, but I knew you would have the baby once you discovered you were."

He watched the anger in her face and was irritated that the plan was backfiring. This wasn't going the way he had it planned at all. He opened his arms, "You should be happy. I want you back and will raise the baby as my own. We're supposed to spend the rest of our lives together."

Karen had been pacing and stopped dead in her tracks.

"What?"

"Baby, let me show you how much I love you. I messed up. I promise I won't do anything like that again. I will love you the way you deserved to be loved."

Her eyes sparked in anger. She clenched her jaw and shook her head.

David saw the fire there that he always loved. Holding his breath, he prayed for an acceptance to his proposal. She would understand and the anger would disappear. "Well, believe it. I do love you and will do anything to get you back."

"You are a very sick man, David. Besides, you seemed to have forgotten another option that I had. Considering how successful you are as a lawyer, I'm surprised you missed something so obvious." Crossing her arms, she arched an eyebrow. "I can't marry you David. I'm already married."

David stood flabbergasted with his mouth opening and closing. He watched her turn and walk away. Tears misted in his eyes as he realized that his one and only true love belonged to another man. Feeling defeated, he wanted to shout and deny what she had told him.

Realizing he was in the middle of a hospital, he cleared his clogged throat, straightened his slumped shoulders, adjusted his tie, and tugged on his jacket. A smile slowly came to his lips as he rolled the tension out of his neck. Speaking quietly to himself, "No need to worry, a marriage under those circumstances and so quickly arranged would never last. I'll just wait until she divorces the loser. Then she'll belong to me."

Karen was furious, at David and herself. How convenient that she brought up the fact that she was married when she was denying it to Bonnie for the last few months. She realized that she had backtracked and quickly entered the doctor's break room. How dare he! That son of a, son of a...that...that... "Bastard!" She screamed.

How could he be so stupid, inconsiderate, and arrogant? That idiot has no idea what he has done! How dare he put holes in the prophylactics and intentionally get her pregnant? What kind of a warped mind did he have that even made him think she would marry him? Why had he been so sure of himself? Was she that easy for him to control, to manipulate?

It had been so long since she had seen Standing Deer. She needed him and missed him. How will he feel about the baby? Will he still love me and want me?

She closed her eyes as the beeper went off. Rubbing her forehead, she temporarily stilled the anger and roiling emotions. Her personal problems would have to wait. She walked to the break room phone to continue with her day.

Standing Deer rode into the village with the band of warriors. Victory had been theirs but with many unfortunate injuries. He looked over at his good friend, Two Feathers, fearing his injuries may be fatal. Standing Deer didn't want to lose his life-long friend. Hopefully Sitting Bull or Spirit of the Mountain would be able to heal his wounds.

A crowd had surrounded the warriors, the cries of the women sounded muffled, and far away. Distracted in search of his wife, he scanned the village, hoping she would be here and not in her magical world.

Silently, he looked into Laughing Flower's eyes and saw the sadness and fear of losing her love reflected back at him. Carefully and with complete caution to avoid the wounds, he picked up Two Feather's and carried the warrior into his lodge. Immediately he and Laughing Flower tended to his friend's wounds.

Guilt flushed throughout his inner being like a plague. They had argued intensely. If it hadn't been for him, Two Feather's wouldn't have been injured. Two Feather's had told Standing Deer that he wasn't paying attention to what was going on around them and if he didn't be careful his foolish behavior would get them all killed.

Two Feather's scolded him as if he was a child, telling him a five-year-old would be able to track him and find him. Standing Deer hadn't realized he'd been so careless. His mind was on Spirit of the Mountain so much lately. Distraction out in the wilderness was a deadly mistake. He knew better than to allow his mind to wander.

He closed his eyes, remembering that fateful moment. They were squatting behind some bushes, watching and waiting for the white men to show themselves. Two Feathers was talking to him, never raising his voice to his good friend. If Standing Deer had been paying attention to his tone of voice, he would have realized that there was concern and not criticism.

Anger controlling his actions and words, Standing Deer accused Two Feathers of not being a true friend. Like an ignorant fool, he exposed himself as he went to move away from the cutting words and accusations. Immediately, Two Feather's realized what he had done and jumped on Standing Deer to pull him down, taking the bullet that was aimed for Standing Deer.

Standing Deer prayed to the Great Spirit, asking him to keep his friend alive and not die because of his foolishness. He looked over to Laughing Flower and asked her forgiveness. Laughing Flower watched Standing Deer's expressions of pain as he spoke to her of how Two Feather's had become injured.

"Standing Deer, you are his blood brother. You must forgive yourself. Two Feathers will not blame you. He will always love you."

Standing Deer nodded his head in acceptance, her kind words easing his guilt.

"You have not asked about Spirit of the Mountain. She is on your mind, as well."

Standing Deer frowned and nodded his head again. "Yes, she is in my thoughts. It seems I cannot think of anything else."

"What bothers you, my friend?"

"I wonder if she hates me for forcing her to marry me. Maybe I should have waited until she was willing."

"It is our way. You were living as man and wife already. You didn't force her into anything."

"It isn't her way. We didn't consider Spirit of the Mountain's feelings on the matter." Standing Deer sighed.

"She loves you. She must live by our laws if she is to live with us. And you shall live by her laws, if you are to live in her world."

"Spirit of the Mountain doesn't want me there. She has told me that much."

Laughing Flower was baffled. It didn't make sense. Why wouldn't she want her husband with her? She recalled the last few months and the time Spirit of the Mountain was in the village. Spirit of the Mountain watched constantly for Standing Deer's arrival, never letting her eyes stray from the entrance of the camp for long.

She could see Standing Deer's heart ached to be with his wife. Was Spirit of the Mountain still fighting her love for Standing Deer? Their world couldn't be that different to make it impossible to be together as man and wife. Could it? She, like everyone else, was very curious about Spirit of the Mountain's world.

"Is her world that different from ours, Standing Deer?"

Smiling, he recalled his adventure in the land Spirit of the Mountain called Florida. This Florida was a complicated world and could cause problems in their life-circle. But if Spirit of the Mountain was willing, they could make their lives together happy and prosperous. He would enjoy being there again as long as it wasn't a permanent situation.

"Yes, it is very different. I cannot speak of her world but I can tell you that it has as much magic as there are stars."

Her eyes widened in wonder, thunderstruck at the description of so much magic. "You jest, Standing Deer."

How could one live with so much magic? No wonder Spirit of the Mountain was so powerful. She recalled a time when she had accidentally seen Spirit of the Mountain moving arrows up and down in the air by just pointing at them. It scared her that she could move objects without touching them.

A sadness and emptiness consumed him as he looked at his friend dying on the buffalo mat and ached for his arms to hold his wife.

Sitting Bull entered the lodge with his medicine bag in hand. Standing Deer allowed Sitting Bull to take his place. He watched silently, as the medicine man tended to the wounds of his blood brother. After a length of time, he completed his task and there wasn't a thing to do but wait. Both Sitting Bull and Standing Deer left the lodge together. There was much to do and a meeting had been called.

Sitting Bull touched his arm. "I have good news for you my friend. Your wife will be arriving soon."

Looking toward his lodge and then at the entrance of the village, Spirit of the Mountain was nowhere in sight. Puzzled, he turned to question Sitting Bull and saw the laughter in his eyes.

"It seems that when she has been gone from our village for any length of time, she goes to her cave that Jumping Bull spoke of. Her horse leaves the camp to bring her to us. If you look for yourself, you will see that it has left the grazing grounds."

Standing Deer was far from surprised. He had seen Spirit of the Mountain disappear into thin air, calling a horse to come and get her was minor magic.

Karen was tired of seeing the vast prairie land before her eyes. When was she going to find Yankton? It was supposed to be the capital of Dakota Territory during this time. Yankton was where she had to buy land in the Dakota Territory.

She laughed as she recalled accusing the first dealer she spoke to of selling her fake money. How was she supposed to know they actually had three dollar and seven dollar bills in those days...these days? Oh, whatever! She sighed heavily. She wasn't sure how to think sometimes. Was it past or present? If you are living in the past, was it considered present? She shook her head in dismay. It was easier to think that a three dollar bill actually existed.

There was more gold in her satchel than cash. She studied cash and land values the night before she arrived back in the Dakota Territory. The gold she had taken from the Black Hills. She didn't do any actual digging but knew that it was still wrong of her to take it. After the rain storm, the gold rocks and pebbles were lying there, scattered on the ground and easy for her to take. She silently thanked her parents for taking her on a gold mine tour when she was younger.

The three dollar bill was unusual. It had a maiden sitting on a pile of coins with what appeared to be a spear in her hand. Behind her on the left, was a picture of George Washington. To the right and just a bit behind the maiden was a plaque. An eagle stood on the plaque with its wings spread wide. The large three in the middle of the bill made it quite easy to identify as a three dollar bill. The remaining three corners had the number three in them as well. The scrollwork on the bills was so intricate it was hard to believe they were capable of doing that kind of detail.

She wasn't sure if the seven dollar bills were confederate money or not. The dealer said that they weren't. She was hesitant to buy them since a bank in Virginia issued them in 1861. The center of these bills has horses playing in a field near a creek. Behind them is a drawing of a train. In each corner, a seven encircled by scrollwork that the dealer said had been machine engraved.

She had to keep it all a secret from Standing Deer and his people. Lord knows how they would react if they knew where she had gotten it. How would the Lakota feel about her taking anything from the Sacred Hills? She doubted they would be happy about it, recalling the anger coming from Crazy Horse and his bitter attitude toward whites.

She couldn't let that stop her. She was happy with the money she had bought, and nervous about the way she had taken the gold. It will make things easier and her plans should fall into place. Now that there was a baby involved, it was that much more important she purchase land in this wilderness.

Her son or daughter will be raised in the modern world. She will not allow the death and devastation of the Lakota Nation to hurt the children. She would try her best to preserve anything she could for the Lakota.

Karen caressed her stomach. When he or she becomes an adult, she knew she would have to let him choose their own path. In the meantime, she will not allow the chance of the child's life to be destroyed by greedy and selfish white men.

As she followed the river southward, Karen finally arrived in the settlement of Yankton. Although it appeared to be what they would call a thriving river port, it was out in the middle of nowhere. She was expecting some kind of warning that a town was nearby but it just appeared. She looked around at the log buildings and wooden structures and realized she was seeing the real thing. This wasn't a restoration and re-creation of an old western town. This was an old western town.

It wasn't difficult to find the bank. Once finished with that business, he sent her in the direction of the mayor's office with an application for a land grant in her hand. It appeared her timing was perfect. A Mr. Leavenworth was in town visiting the mayor at that very moment. He was the one who signed the land grants. She wouldn't have to spend a dime!

Karen wondered if it was the same Leavenworth that she had read about in history. She searched her memory but couldn't quite recall. She rode past a hotel and decided to get a room.

A boy passed by, "Excuse me young man, could you tell me where I can bring my horse to be taken care of properly?"

The boy, about twelve years, had golden blonde hair pulled back into a ponytail. His eyes were a watery blue with dark circles underneath, showing he had not gotten much sleep lately.

He shoved his hands into his pockets and shuffled his feet. "Why ma'am," he drawled. "Rat down that at Mr. Sam's." He pointed with his nose. "I can take it far ya."

Thanking him, she pressed a coin in his hand bidding him to do well. She asked that he return her horse to her first thing in the morning. His eyes doubled in size when he saw the coin.

"Thank ya ma'am. Thank ya. I make sure ya harse is tooken real good care of. Good as gold, I's shores will."

She watched as he took the horse and smiled as she entered the hotel. She obviously gave him much more than he expected. No harm done. He'll make sure the horse is taken "good care of, good as gold."

After she paid for her room, she requested a bath and thanked God she had been smart enough to pack one of those long gowns. Quick as humanly possible, she was bathed and dressed looking like the grandest southern belle ever to set foot in the west.

It was well worth the effort. Mr. Leavenworth was talkative and became excited when Karen inquired if he was related to the Leavenworth family from Fort Leavenworth. Proud of his heritage, he stuck out his chest and said Col. Henry Leavenworth was his grandfather.

He was more than happy to grant her one thousand acres instead of the customary five hundred. In his mind, she was a Southerner trying to start a new life now that the north had destroyed her land. Inviting her to dine with him, she couldn't refuse his offer. Thankfully, Mr. Leavenworth was a Southern sympathizer. He had been quite generous with the land grant.

Morning came quickly and she was on her way. The plans were now in motion.

Chapter Fourteen

Standing Deer couldn't wait another week. Something was wrong. He could feel it in his bones. Sitting Bull had said she would arrive soon but a week had passed. Even he had been watching the entrance to the village and worrying. Two Feathers was still deathly ill. He had to find her.

Standing Deer headed toward the cave near the hot springs. He had to be cautious now that the Great White War was over. There were many white men and black men going throughout their lands. If any of these white men harmed Spirit of the Mountain then he would have their scalps. If they harmed her in anyway, he might even use methods from the Scili and use them for torture and human sacrifice.

Days later, he retracted his steps forever searching for a sign of the woman he loved. Spying a lone traveler, he recognized the stance of the man on the horse. It was John Colby, Little Fox's husband.

John had recently returned to the village. Now that he was back, Sunshine in the Morning was once again in Standing Deer's lodge. While John was fighting in the white man's war, Sunshine in the Morning stayed with her sister to keep her company and help the time go by quickly.

The two men rode silently to the village, each deep in their own thoughts. As they entered the village, a young brave yelled to Standing Deer.

"She is here, Spirit of the Mountain has arrived!"

Standing Deer dismounted from his horse and ran, with John Colby's at his heels to the center of the village where a group of people gathered. He picked up Spirit of the Mountain and swung her around before he gave her a kiss that caused the group to cheer and tease.

John stood by patiently waiting while Little Fox stood next to him in silence. This Spirit of the Mountain was indeed very beautiful and she had the people in the palm of her hands. It would be his pleasure to humble the wench in front of these naive and ignorant Indians. Standing next to Spirit of the Mountain was another exquisite looking creature. He wondered where this white woman came from as well, and if she supposedly had magical powers from the Great Spirit.

Standing Deer looked over to John Colby and called him over to introduce Spirit of the Mountain and her friend, Bonnie.

John approached the group. He had also been out searching for the white woman before he spotted Standing Deer on the horse. The whole village was in love with her. Curiosity had gotten the best of him. This woman had to be something special if she had these heathens thinking she was some kind of child of God. What did she do, tell them she is the sister of Jesus? He'd get down to the bottom of it all. No wench was going to play witch with him. He knew how to tame a woman.

Karen watched silently as a young man in a confederate uniform, limped slowly over to greet her. His eyes were a steel gray and his dark brown curly hair stuck out from under his hat. The man was very thin, tall and looked sickly...definitely war worn. The young man had a distinctive frown curling around his eyes with a flash of sparkling insanity. There was an instantaneous dislike of him the minute she looked into his face.

"John Colby has recently returned from the Great White War. He fought for freedom and has returned a great and honorable warrior."

Karen raised her eyebrow. "It is a pleasure to meet you, Mr. Colby. How long were you in the war?"

"I've been gone for over two years and am very glad to be back with my Sioux family." Responded Colby as he roughly pulled Little Fox into his embrace.

Karen realized immediately that something was seriously wrong. Little Fox had never mentioned a husband and she didn't look pleased that Colby had arrived safely back to the village. She was stiff with tension. Perhaps Little Fox thought her husband was dead. The Lakota don't speak of their dead, out of respect for their souls. She had thought Little Fox was interested in Sleeping Elk but her shyness stopped her from pursuing him. Now Karen understood it was because of Colby.

"I'm sure you are happy and relieved to be here. Perhaps during the meal you could entertain us with some of your stories of the war."

"I would be delighted. Now, if you will excuse me, I would like to spend some time with Little Fox."

Karen watched as he walked away, wondering why she didn't trust the man. A few feet to her right stood Crazy Horse and Sleeping Elk, watching with obvious anger in their eyes. Trouble was brewing.

Sitting Bull and Standing Deer took the opportunity to whisk Karen away and bring her to Two Feathers. Sitting Bull's work on Two Feather's was meticulous. No one could have done a better job under the circumstances.

He had lost a lot of blood. He couldn't get a transfusion but she could give him vitamins and iron pills, have Sitting Bull make an infusion that could build his immune system. Her hands were tied; all she could do was pray. She instructed Sitting Bull and Laughing Flower on how often to give the pills, requested he concoct an herbal potion, and then solemnly left the lodge.

After their meals most of the village went about their business, few stayed to listen to the stories of the white soldier. Karen saw Crazy Horse and Sleeping Elk across the village close enough to hear, ever watchful but keeping a safe distance. Karen and Bonnie seized the opportunity to approach the group as Colby was telling his tales.

"...That was a rough one. By capturing Vicksburg, Grant was able to have complete control of the Mississippi. After that Bragg made a lot of mistakes in the war and was pushed back over to Chattanooga." Colby looked around at the faces of the people around him and continued with his war stories.

"After Bragg was defeated, Johnston took over the command. Because he needed time to strengthen his troops, Johnston stayed at Dalton. While Johnston was in Dalton, Sherman captured Atlanta but the Confederates escaped.

Johnston's command was taken over by Hood, who was forced to evacuate Dalton. We made our ways around for a few months until we were delayed because of supplies that was in Florence. The last battle I was in was the one where my legs were injured, that was in December past. We were in Nashville waiting on troops from Texas when Thomas defeated Hood's troops in a bloody ruthless battle. Hood managed to escape over to Tennessee. I was injured and in an army hospital. The next thing I know, the war was over."

Colby looked up to see Karen intently watching him. She was aware of how cautious he was about not informing the Lakota whose command he actually fought under. He spoke of the war as if he watched it from behind the scenes, as a spectator.

"You fought for the North, Mr. Colby?" Karen inquired. I detect an accent that's a bit familiar, more southern."

John drawled. "I fought for freedom of choice, madam."

"If you fought for freedom of choice, Mr. Colby, then why do you wear the confederate uniform?"

The village was silent. Listening to the conversation, not knowing what to expect, they were surprised by the tone in Spirit of the Mountain's voice. Standing Deer took a step back to listen to the conversation when Crazy Horse took Bonnie's arm and moved her behind him placing himself next to Spirit of the Mountain.

It was obvious to her that Crazy Horse never liked the white man Little Fox married. Chances are he couldn't put his finger on why but went with his instincts.

Anger crossed Colby's face, he didn't hide his dislike of Spirit of the Mountain's questions. "I told you, I fought for freedom...of choice."

"Why did it take you so long to return to the Lakota if the war was over for you last December, it's October...almost November, isn't it? And Mr. Colby, whose freedom of choice did you fight for, certainly not the black man's or the Indian's? If you fought with the Confederate army then you fought for slavery and succession. You didn't fight for freedom...of choice, as you say."

"Being a woman, I will acknowledge that you don't have the capacity or the ability to understand the degrees of warfare or governmental politics. I don't believe you understand or comprehend what the war was truly about. The southern states wanted the freedom of choice. Standing Deer, do you not have control over your wife?"

Standing Deer's eyes blazed with anger. "My wife is my equal and may speak her mind."

"But I do know what I'm talking about. I completely understand what the Civil War was all about. I know exactly what the south was fighting for." Karen paused and looked around. "You sir, failed to specify which side you fought for and the commands under which officers."

Pointing at him, "History states that Grant took control over Vicksburg. He fought for the North, the Federal or the Union army, whichever you prefer to call them. Bragg and Johnston both fought for the Confederate armies. Sherman did indeed capture Atlanta but he fought for the Union.

Thomas, under Sherman's command, was left behind to fight Hood, and Thomas was the one to defeat your confederate troops in December."

She smiled and crossed her arms while she tapped her foot. She was more than willing to play the devil's advocate. History was one of her favorite subjects. "You fought for the Confederate side. You fought for slavery and succession. Mr. Colby, you have deceived these good people into believing that you fought for freedom."

Colby stood up in anger, grabbed Little Fox, and pulled her to her feet. "I see you are a northern sympathizer. You are a traitor to our southern heritage, as well as a deceitful wench. You may have the Indians fooled with your witchcraft and sorcery but you have not fooled me."

Karen looked around and watched the curious stares from her friends. Now wasn't the time or the place to pursue this disagreement. She hadn't noticed until then, but Crazy Horse had placed his hand on her shoulder. It was a sign for all to see that he would back her up, if he was needed.

"No man regardless of the color of his skin should be a slave to anyone. Believe what you wish about me, but I wonder whose side you will choose when the white man comes to conquer the Sioux territory? Where will your heart lie then, Mr. Colby?"

"You are a stupid wench. The white man will not come here, you have these peaceful people worried unnecessarily." Red-faced from anger, Colby hissed at her and spit on the ground.

Abruptly he pulled Little Fox's arm and walked away.

Crazy Horse whispered to Spirit of the Mountain. "You have made an enemy today."

Karen looked at Crazy Horse and gave him a half-hearted smile as he spoke in hushed tones with Standing Deer. She didn't truly believe John Colby was wrong in fighting for what he believed. She just didn't agree with slavery or his deception. She found it hard to believe that he would fight for slavery when he knew how much the Lakota believed in freedom. They didn't believe in slavery. They believed no man or creature, big or small, should be a slave.

Did Colby know that they had taken Indian's from all different tribes and used them for slaves as well as the blacks? He had to know. His family probably owned slaves.

Colby led them to believe that he fought for freedom, conveniently omitting to explain to the Lakota whose side he had fought for. He was a man that will show his true colors soon enough. Hopefully no one will be hurt. Karen would have to watch out for this man. Crazy Horse warned her wisely. She had made an enemy today.

Bonnie shook Karen's arm. "Why did you intentionally bait him? This is so exciting! Who was the Indian standing next to Mr. Colby and who was next to you?"

Bonnie was so excited her eyes rushed around the village in a frenzy trying to absorb everything all at once. As usual she was spouting out so many questions it made Karen's head spin.

"Slow down. You will learn more if you stay silent. Silence is a virtue in the eyes of the Lakota. You must use patience. If you start talking when it isn't your turn, you will offend someone. The Lakota believe that silence is the complete balance of the mind, body, and soul. It is a cornerstone of their being."

"Who's that talking to Standing Deer?"

"*Tashunca Uitco*, Crazy Horse."

Bonnie's eyes grew as large as golf balls. "THE Crazy Horse?!" Her eyes darted quickly to where Standing Deer and Crazy Horse stood talking. "That's the infamous Crazy Horse? Why he's just a boy! He's the one who is determined to hate and destroy all white men?"

"Hush Bonnie, some of these people understand English. He is already considered a man in his people's eyes. He's older than he looks. This is 1865. He doesn't become chief until later. It will take him years to learn the war techniques that will make him the famous man he was...is...oh...you know what I mean."

Bonnie was staring at Crazy Horse. "So what is he really like? Is he like the way history has described him?"

"Bonnie, history describes a man in his late twenties and older. He is still growing into what he will be."

Biting her lip, she continued. "Some of the things they wrote about him are true. Crazy Horse is an extremely intelligent person with a big, generous heart. He isn't a guiltless, uncaring savage. He will change some when he goes to war. Remember that he goes to war to defend his family and country. What man has not changed because of war? This is his home. He will not want it taken away from him and neither will the rest of the Sioux Indians."

Karen started walking toward Standing Deer's tent. "The Lakota are pure family-oriented. You will soon be very impressed by their attitudes toward family and friends. Keep your eyes open and your mouth closed. Don't speak unless spoken to. Otherwise, you may offend them. Your personality is a little bit more outgoing than they are accustomed to. Be careful. The Lakota believe that when a person talks too much, they have nothing to say."

"I know. I talk too much and the Indian's don't care for it. Whose lodge is that?" She pointed to the largest one in the village.

"That's Jumping Bull's and next to his lodge is Sitting Bull's. This is Standing Deer's lodge."

"It isn't far from Sitting Bull's at all. It's just one lodge away. Does that mean Standing Deer is important in the village, also?" Bonnie inquired.

Karen nodded her head. "He is highly respected among his people. Standing Deer has accomplished many coups and is a member of the Strong Heart Warrior Society."

"What is...?"

"Bonnie, please. Let's just go sit inside and relax for a while. We'll have some tea or coffee. There's plenty of time to answer questions and a lot of them will be answered if you watch the people and everything around you."

Hours passed as they spoke about the Lakota and Karen's pregnancy. While they waited for Standing Deer, there were several interruptions from women and men coming to the lodge to welcome her back. Bonnie was amazed at how quickly Karen had learned the language.

Karen laughed when Bonnie commented on her accomplishment. "I have the vocabulary of a child and I still pronounce some words incorrectly, but the people are very patient."

Standing Deer entered the lodge and spoke of how he would like to take them out for a ride the next day. He felt Bonnie should see the prairie and all of the Great Spirit's wonders. Bonnie offered to leave so the two could be alone, but Standing Deer replied that he would like to take Karen for a walk along the river.

Smiling, the two left the lodge. It felt good to be together. There had been too much lost time and much to discuss. Karen wasn't sure where to begin. She believed Standing Deer was waiting for her to begin speaking first.

Watching her silently, he could see there was much weighing on her mind and it wasn't the deceiving Colby. They would have to keep their eyes on that man. He had deceived them greatly, leading them to believe that he fought for the freedom of people.

"Standing Deer, I guess the best way to tell you is to come right out and say it." Karen inhaled deeply. "I'm ihlusaka...pregnant."

He howled in joy, picked her up, and swirled her around, hugging her so tight she could just barely breathe. He was ecstatic. "The Great Spirit has blessed us with a child." He was thankful to Him.

"Please stop. This wasn't supposed to happen. That's why I insisted that we use the prophylactics. David did it. He..."

"WHAT!" Standing Deer roared. "David got you pregnant?"

This wasn't coming out right! "Listen, please. David had taken the prophylactics and put holes in all of them so I would conceive. He did it intentionally. David claims he loves me and believed that if I got pregnant by you that you would desert me. Then he would marry me and raise the child as his own."

"That is stupid. That is the last thing you should do if you truly love someone."

"Marry them?" Karen asked with a twinkle in her eyes.

"No." He grunted. "Get them pregnant on purpose with someone else's child!" He turned and looked at her and saw she had been teasing. He smiled and gave her a hug.

"Well, what shall we do? We needed to decide how to live anyway. Now we just include our child in the plans."

"Actually..." Karen hesitated. It was going to be hard to tell him. "It is a harder decision because of the child. If it was just the two of us, it would be different. We probably could have worked out the difference in our two worlds. With a child, it's too complicated. The child cannot be raised with two separated lives. The child will have to be raised in one world only."

Standing Deer nodded in approval. "I completely agree. There are plenty of women in the village to help raise the child when you aren't here. All will love the child as if it was their own."

"No! That isn't what I meant! The child will live in my world. It will be safer and he will receive the proper education."

"He is Lakota and will be raised as a Lakota. My word is final. He must learn to live as one with the Earth. He needs to learn the ways of the Great Spirit and what is expected of him as a warrior. He must learn to wanase, hunt buffalo.

"What if it is a girl? Besides, neither one of them is going to be raised as a warrior. They can be taught all of those things in my world." She crossed her arms. "The child will be raised in my world."

"No, I have a right to decide what to do with our child."

"You have a right to tell me what you want." She pushed her hair back, combing it with her fingers. "I have the final decision. The child will be raised in my world and you can't stop me."

Karen turned to walk away when Standing Deer grabbed her arm.

"*Mitawin, niye namlasva*!" My wife, you break my heart!

Tears streaming down her face, she yanked her arm out of his grip. Karen replied with determination that would move a mountain. "I will not allow the child to live two separate lives. If you choose to help raise your child in my world, that is agreeable. If you insist that the child live in yours, you will never see the child again."

With that said she abruptly walked away. Bonnie was already half asleep when she arrived back at the lodge. Karen laid on Standing Deer's mat. She could smell his manly odor as she tossed and turned restlessly. Arguing with him was futile, regardless of how much she felt she was right. It was a long time before sleep claimed her.

The next day at the river, Karen and Bonnie had heard rumors that Sleeping Elk had called out Colby to kicie conape, fight to the death. Colby was nowhere to be found. As far as the Lakota were concerned, Colby was dead along with his woyuonihan, his honor.

As the women approached Standing Deer's lodge, they saw he was ready and waiting. He had not forgotten his promise to Bonnie to take her to see the prairie lands.

They rode along the river for about an hour and proceeded toward the prairies. Bonnie was surprised to see the abundance of golden colored prairie dogs. She spotted an osprey as Standing Deer was pointing out some black-footed ferrets scurrying around one of the prairie dog nests.

Standing Deer explained to Bonnie how the prairie dogs were much like any other creature on earth. They lived in colonies, living in the underground, using the earth as their homes, for protection against predators and the elements.

As they approached the animals, Bonnie heard a high-pitched chirping sound that seemed to be a form of communication that danger may be approaching. They watched and listened as the sounds became louder. The pitch increased higher as the three moved closer to their nests. Bonnie stared as the creatures dove into their homes, and peaked their heads out to watch the three intruders go by on their horses.

Standing Deer explained to Bonnie how snakes and badgers hunt the prairie dogs and how the circle of life includes all of the Great Spirit's creatures. He told them how black widow spiders will live near the entrance of the burrowed homes and one must be extremely careful when they upset a nest.

As they rode on, Bonnie saw and understood why Karen loved the Dakota Territory so much. It would be easy to live here for the rest of her life. But that was her, not Karen.

Not many words had passed between Standing Deer and Karen. Uncomfortable because of the unnatural silence, Bonnie had started talking about the land Karen had been granted and how she had applied for a job on the Lakota reservation in South Dakota. By Karen and Standing Deer's reactions, Bonnie had realized too late that Karen had not told him yet. With dread, she quickly clamped her mouth shut as tight as possible.

The last twenty minutes back to the village passed in dead, cold silence.

Chapter Fifteen

When John Colby finally reached the Black Hills, he was still blind with fury. Thank God those heathens didn't chase after him. That wench Karen ruined years of planning. If she had just minded her own business, he could have stayed with the Indians until he had enough gold to live the rest of his life in luxury.

Colby shook his head in disgust. His plans started going wrong with the loss of the Civil War. They had to win that war, how would he be able to own the biggest plantation in all of Georgia without slaves? Now he would have to pay people to work for him. Instead of having the protection of the Sioux, now he would have to mine for the gold and watch his back, all because of that high and mighty wench.

He'll get his gold. Then, he'll get the wench. She will pay. He will make her pay if it's the last thing he does.

Standing Deer entered the lodge with the fury of a bull. Bonnie quickly excused herself, practically running out the door.

"Why did you buy land?" He growled.

"I didn't buy land, they gave me a grant for it. I own the land but it didn't cost me anything. When someone puts their land up for sale, I can buy more."

"It isn't our way. We cannot sell or own the land the Great Spirit has given us. No one can. It isn't their right. It belongs to all, not just one person."

Karen explained. "I did it to help. It was the only way I knew how without interfering with the future."

"It isn't our way!"

"It's the white man's way and I'm doing what I can. Your way will change. This was the only solution I could come up with at the time."

Standing Deer was frustrated. He knew deep in his heart that she was right. Even though he didn't like it, for the time being he was going to have to accept it.

"We have more important things to discuss."

Standing Deer raised his eyebrows in question. "What?"

"The baby. We seem to disagree on what is best for our relationship and this child's upbringing."

"But we do agree to a point." Standing Deer poured himself a cup of tea and offered some to Karen. "A child must be with both parents. Do you disagree with that?"

"No. That is very important."

"And you also agree that a child should receive the benefits of what both parents can teach the child."

"Yes, of course."

"Then our disagreement yesterday was unnecessary, the child will live in both worlds."

"No."

Standing Deer sighed. "My love, you just agreed what was best for the child and now you say no."

"Please understand. Our life is complicated enough for us as it is, living in two separate worlds. If it was just the two of us, then we could probably make it work but with a child it would be too difficult. The child can learn from you without living in the village. I cannot allow the child to live in two separate worlds. It would be too confusing and frustrating."

"I will not be able to teach him the ways of the Lakota in your world of concrete buildings!"

"I agree, wholeheartedly. That is why I have applied for a job at the Pine Ridge Reservation."

"The Pine Ridge Reservation? But you are happy with the job you have now. Why change?"

"For you and the child. We will be living on Sioux land and you can teach him everything he needs to know. The only difference is that it will be in my world and not yours."

"Why leave the work that you love? You will be taking a chance that you will not be happy with the new job. How can he learn the ways of the Lakota on a reservation?"

"It's safer! I will not have my child's life taken away by some greedy white man who wants to hunt for gold."

"I will not live on a reservation! I will not allow my child to live on one. The Lakota are free and it must stay that way."

Karen lifted both hands and started rubbing her temples. This conversation was heading for a brick wall.

"Then we will live near the reservation."

"No. What you plan is unnecessary. The child can learn both worlds without living in or near a reservation. I don't want our child living near those pathetic people who gave up their freedom."

"They aren't pathetic!" Putting her open hand toward him, "Maybe you could find a way to help them if you feel there is such a great need!"

"No. They made their choice. My child will learn the ways of the Lakota as I did."

She growled in frustration. "What do you mean they made their choice? They didn't have a choice. No, Standing Deer. No, plain and simple. I will not allow my child to be raised in a world where the only future is death and destruction." Karen pushed herself up and turned to Standing Deer before leaving the lodge. "You have no choice. The child will not live in this world."

Karen found Bonnie with Laughing Flower and Two Feathers. He was recuperating slower than she had hoped but he would live.

She had decided to leave now and not wait any longer. Karen tried to find Standing Deer but he was nowhere around. It was a tearful good-bye with Sitting Bull and Jumping Bull. They didn't want to believe that she wouldn't be returning.

As they left the village, Karen turned and waved a last good-bye before she and Bonnie headed toward the cave where she first came to this land. Standing Deer's horse was missing and she hoped that he wouldn't try to stop her. She didn't see was the lone proud warrior hidden in the woods, silently watching them leave with tears in his eyes.

Karen was driving in a rental car down State Highway 240, the Badlands Loop. The correspondence between her and James Black Elk took months before an interview was finally set up, red tape, red tape, and more red tape. With the baby being due in a month, she was lucky the doctor approved of the plane trip.

She needed the drive through the scenic route of the Badlands. For the last few months Bonnie had nagged her to no-ends about how wrong she was about her decision with Standing Deer. Her nagging caused doubts to flourish in her mind. Maybe being so close to his land she would be able to think clearly. She needed to be as near to him as she could. Her heart ached with the pain of a lost love.

Karen still believed her decision was the best for the child. With Bonnie's constant nagging, it made her question herself. Was she being the inconsiderate, cold, and callous person Bonnie accused her of? Was she really rejecting the one and only true love that can only be found deep in the soul? Her mind raged in its own personal war.

Deciding to play tourist, she wanted to enjoy the area. She was here for the first time and planned to see Mt. Rushmore and the Crazy Horse Monument while she could.

Driving on 16-A, Karen could see through the trees and got a quick glance of the monument. When she finally reached the sight, she stood in awe and stared at the sixty foot faces. Realizing time was getting away from her, she started toward the Crazy Horse Monument before she checked into her hotel in Custer.

She hadn't known they were creating a monument for Crazy Horse until she had become involved with the Lakota. When she arrived at the unfinished monument, Karen learned that the sculptor had started carving Crazy Horse somewhere around 1947.

The Lakota Chief Henry Standing Bear had wanted all people to know that the Native American's also had great heroes. His requested project was accepted. The monument was still being sculpted, even after the death of Ziolkowski. His wife and family have kept it going. The Crazy Horse Monument will be the largest known statue in the world. When it is finished its size will be estimated at 531 feet high and 641 feet long.

Karen felt strange and awkward. To know Crazy Horse personally as she does and to see his face carved in stone was eerie. Chills went up her spine.

There was a slight wonder as to why Red Cloud or Sitting Bull had not been chosen, but she dismissed the question as quickly as it came. All were great heroes to the Sioux Nation. She was sure it was hard to choose one to represent them all.

The night went by quickly. She had the best sleep she could recall in months. As she headed south and turned onto the lone road heading for the reservation, Karen felt a presence. She could hear drums beating and the sounds of a familiar Lakota ritual song. Looking around, she couldn't see anyone. She couldn't shake the feeling that she was being watched. The song stayed in her mind as she drove on.

Some homes weren't suitable for people to live in, yet she watched children playing in the yards. It didn't settle well for her. She felt she had entered a third world.

Relieved, she saw the building she was looking for as she slowly pulled the car up to the side and placed it carefully in park. Awkward with her added weight, she slowly exited the car. Two teenagers were leaning against the building, silently watching her brush her hair.

As she walked up the steps, she noted the scarves sticking out of their pockets; both were blue. She wondered if the stories were true that gangs were now among the reservations.

Smiling at them with a cheerful, "Good morning." She looked into their eyes, both boys leaned forward, dumbfounded. Their mouths dropped open.

The taller one whispered something to the other boy and he took off running. With the look of shock still on his face, he opened the door for her and let her in. Then he turned and ran in the same direction as the other boy.

Puzzled, Karen shook her head. Their reaction to her was quite strange. As she entered the building, she looked around at the various pictures on the wall. There was a quiet conversation going on between the woman behind the desk and a gentleman who was leaning over her reading a paper.

They both looked up at the same time and both stared at her in the same manner as the young boys.

"Hello," Karen said as she put her hand out to shake theirs, "I'm..."

The woman jumped up, "Yes, yes, we know who you are. I'll tell him you're here." She ran to a closed door, not turning the knob fast enough, she bumped into it. She turned to Karen, apologized, and then entered the other room.

Karen heard muffled voices as she nodded a hello to the gentleman who stood staring at her without saying a word. She wondered what was wrong with them. Why were they looking at her in such a strange way?

The woman came out, escorted her into the other room, and shut the door behind her. The man's head was bent down signing some papers. She took the short moment to glance at the pictures on the walls. There were many pictures of Indians and villages showing the old ways of life. She saw a quite pleasant picture of Red Cloud laughing. As she looked at the picture behind the desk, she realized it was Sitting Bull, with a woman standing near him in the background. Squinting her eyes to get a better look, she realized the woman was her.

She closed her eyes and inhaled a deep breath. Oh no...

Looking up from his work, he showed no sign of any kind of reaction as the others had given her. Slowly he rose from the desk and just as slowly walked over to her.

Cupping Karen's hand with both of his, he whispered... "Welcome, He Woniya." Spirit of the Mountain.

A Sioux Prayer

Oh Great Spirit,

You have shown me a vision that saddens my heart...

Bless me with the sight of an eagle, the cunning of a fox, the strength of a buffalo, and the wisdom of the wind, so I may defeat my enemy that wants to destroy what you have given your people.

Guide me to teach the young ones your ways, so they will follow the right path...even when they are told it is wrong.

Help me open their arms to your love, so they will not fall prey to the evils of our enemies.

Help me open their arms to your love, so they will not fall prey to the evils of our enemies.

Thank-you Great Spirit, for the life you have given me. I pray that I return your gift of life with honor and love when it is my time to be with you for all eternity.

34611548R00073

Made in the USA
Middletown, DE
28 August 2016